CONDUITS:
The Ballad of Jinx Jenkins

A Storybook for Grownups

J. RYAN SOMMERS

CONDUITS: THE BALLAD OF JINX JENKINS
Transmundane Press, LLC| www.transmundanepress.com
Editor-in-Chief & Co-Publisher: Alisha Chambers
Content Editor & Co-Publisher: Anthony S. Buoni

ISBN-13: 978-0-9984983-3-1
ISBN-10: 0998498335
Worldwide Rights
Created in the United States of America

Cover Design: Hampton J. Lamoureux
Interior Layout: Alisha Chambers
Author Photo: Jackie Ontiveros

DEDICATION

For Lillian,
My Wife, My Life,
My Muse.

CONTENTS

ACKNOWLEDGMENTS

Thank you to every last teacher I ever had (especially the English and Humanities teachers), from Lake Forest High School, the University of Arizona, the University of California Los Angeles, and Columbia College Chicago. You have passed on your knowledge, which is priceless. Thank you to my fraternity brothers and the R.O.C., who helped shape me into the man I am today. Thank you to my friends at SubSun, who have been my guiding light throughout this entire process. May we continue to "level up" for the rest of our lives. An extra special thanks to my family. I assure you, if you see parallels to yourselves, the intention was never meant to be malicious. Extra special thanks as well to Alexis Pride, Sam Weller, RS Deeren, Alex Donnelly, my dogs (Keaton and Gidget), Toni Morison, John Steinbeck, F. Scott Fitzgerald, Clarice Lispector, Ray Bradbury, Alan Moore, Neil Gaiman, Norman Rockwell, Gordon Lightfoot, the Grayfriars Bobby, and so, so many more that influenced the work before you. And lastly to my wife, who put up with my incessant complaints and neurosis throughout this entire process. I love you all.

This is the story of a place, a county in fact, called Green Valley. It follows the lives of various inhabitants and details specific places of special note. It is both magical realism and heavily influenced by parody. Many, but not all, of the stories in this collection are paralleled in other *Conduits* books.

Author's Note to the Reader:
WELCOME TO GREEN VALLEY

It exists in a long-forgotten corner of the American dream. It exits in the soul of every town and every village, every suburb and every city. It exists in twilight—that place between waking and dreaming. If you go looking for it, you will pass it by. To find it, you must forget your way there. A place unlike any other, it saturates your consciousness when you are visiting, and it quickly falls to the back of your memory once you've left. To say you remember it fully is a lie. And to say you have no memory at all would be the same.

We have all been to Green Valley.

Don't you remember?

That strange county, with an over population of trees, gray-green snow, and buildings washed in art. Contained within a tall mountain ridge, Green Valley is inhabited by a great arbor sanctuary, several small villages, and a river that trickles down its spine. The citizenship walks about, stained in a noxious film that intrudes their pores, their hair, and everything they own.

A single road stretches in a large, dented circle—Main Street. It runs through the forest and over mountain cliffs. It weaves its way from oasis to oasis and carries all the hopes and dreams of the people. The only way in or out of town is an entrance and an exit at either end, where upon you'll find yourself back in a thick expanse of trees. Your lone guide, the woven tunnel of branches slinking in a fearful gauntlet through the forest.

The crescent valley is located in the heart of the country. The mountain chain tall and foreboding, verdant and fertile.

It's right there on the map, don't you see?

The valley's mouth runs along the banks of Lake Sibylline—a lake large enough to be a member of the Great Lakes, but separated by land, and therefore, discarded by the public's devotion. Sibylline is the second largest American lake, as well as the second deepest. But when was the last time anybody remembered who came in second?

Along the tortured shores, the people migrate to the metropolis where they find love and hate, work and play, and answer to the god in the crystal tower. But we'll get to that…

Historically, Green Valley is the foremost spawning ground for the mighty North American Jackalope. During monsoons, lightning attacks the land, trees catch fire, and the antlered rodents mate until exhaustion. In spring, when the young follow their loins back home, many a tire is punctured by the razor points of road kill. Some go as far as to worship the vicious beasts, while still others enjoy them with currants and a splash of Worcestershire.

A place like *all* others, it has roads and houses and people and lots and lots of trees. Children go to school. Rush hour is a bitch. And in the summer, cicadas cry with lust. Also a place unlike *any* other, there are heroes and villains, murderers and ghosts, and lots and lots of magic. A boy crows at the sun. Mutants sneak in the shadows. And in the summer, the tired river catches fire and keeps the night at bay.

Consumed by a vast pattern of interconnected circles and tracks and trains, like a snake eating its own tail, the links in the chain glide along in never-ending loops. The valley people ride in the belly of the serpent, moving to and from the city. It was given to them by a madman. He will die for their sins.

A place that God and the Devil forgot, and in their absence, others filled the void. Enacting their will through mediums—conduits to their hope and rage, fear and love, truth, justice, and lust. They will lead a revolution. They will rediscover humanity.

To start our story with "Once upon a time" would be disingenuous. Green Valley exists at all times, which makes that particular adage a bit tricky. Rather, let's say it happened "Once upon a place…" and leave it at that.

Welcome to Green Valley. We've been expecting you.

I.

The smelliest man who ever lived, his scent was enough to turn a cadaver's stomach. Although a simple vagabond, beaten by the worst stones life could throw at him, he was known the valley over as Jinx Jenkins. Hair crusted white in a thick layer of filth, skin ashen and gray-green, like a seasick corpse. The fetid reek of burning bodies, bile, blistering boils, and puss saturated his very being.

His home was the Green Valley Skytram, the great feat of engineering spanning the valley. A tangle of concentric circles, all moving perpetually about the valley floor, along the cliff sides, and through the terrible cosmopolis of Lakeview, the city by the shore.

Jinx had an ability, people said, to cause all manner of destruction and infirmity. A man so unlucky, he made businesses fail, teams loose, and food turn. Babies cried when he came too close. Men and women gasped for air when trapped in his general purlieu, hurrying far from him in search of sanctuary. His mere presence caused people to lose their wallets, miss steps, or trip on the smoothest of surfaces. For this reason, if one realized Jinx was present on their tram, they packed to the opposite side and waited to switch cars at the next station.

This was the situation when Clarion Brightway, a young woman of twenty-three, wearing the bluest dress ever conceived, entered the car off the Jackson Street terminal. She took a single breath of the foul odor permeating the train, and when she recognized poor Jinx, made for the exit. Lucky enough, she escaped before the doors closed, releasing her into the crisp morning city air. But she did not leave the car unimpeded, slipping between the boardwalk and the tram.

As the tram rolled on, the bump it caused in the car woke Jinx from his slumber. He hooted and grumbled before slipping back to sleep.

A SUNNY DAY

Gregg Ryan had developed the sneaking suspicion that he did not matter. His life was made up of tiny boxes and buttons. In the morning, he woke to the exhausted rays collapsing through the blinds. He'd pull them open, revealing the alley and brick wall of the neighboring building. Gregg lived in a laughable one-room studio consisting of a cotbed, a screen embedded into the wall, a console with a multitude of fading colored buttons, a stool, and a slot his meals came from. On the wall hung a framed picture of a beautiful woman he liked to pretend was his mother.

The picture was from a magazine.

Gregg wanted one thing—that someday, the clouds would part, and he might see the bright and shining sun and know the true color of the sky. On the best days, the sky was a tired white. On the worst, it was a green and purple soup that cried. He'd been told the sky was blue, and as a boy believed white and blue were one and the same. But when he learned they were not, he realized he did not know what blue was. Of course, he'd seen pictures and dresses and crayons that all consisted of blue. But he'd never truly comprehended the color.

A perpetual layer of stubble darkened his face, and his stringy hair never stayed the way he wanted it. Gregg pushed the green button on the wall console. Inside, something rattled, then clunked, groaned, and a bowl appeared from the slot.

Despite the number of buttons on the console, Gregg only ever pushed the same four. One for switching on and off the lights. One for switching on and off the screen. One for producing food. And one for keeping the place clean. Beyond that, he had no desire to discover what the other buttons did. Or rather, his fear outweighed his desire.

Gregg walked to work every day, a short trek consisting of two elevators, two right turns and one left, a bridge, three crosswalks, and a turnstile that never seemed to work. Hurried crowds of gray people rushed around him.

He imagined God grew bored painting the blank sky and abandoned it before finishing. The emptiness dulled the colors, making everything appear fake. Yet, little did God realize that his tiny unfinished world had come alive and gone on without him.

He worked in a lonely room with a single desk lamp, which always burned too bright, yet left a majority of the space in abyssal darkness. His skin was pale, his eyes were sunken, and carried a long, lean frame that made him seem taller than he was.

He sat at a desk with a ruddy red button in its center. Gregg's job was simple. In the morning, he pushed the button to start up the Lakeview SkyTram. At night, he pushed it again to end the day's transit. Throughout the day, he stared at a lifeless red bulb that illuminated to indicate a problem with the trains.

There were never any problems with the trains.

One morning, Gregg spotted a girl out of the corner of his eye as she passed him at one of his three crosswalks. He spun to see her again but lost her in the bustling crowd. For the rest of the day, he struggled to remember what she looked like, but all he pictured was a blinding flash of light.

Something different about her.

Something he didn't have words for.

He needed to see her again like lungs needed air or trees needed rain.

The following day, he searched for her again, merely to find a homogenized population of gray faces. His day at work was both tedious and brief while he was consumed by the fading image of the girl.

In his sixteen years as the SkyTram operator, he'd never once met another employee. His sole work companion consisted of a framed picture of Jason Big, President and CEO of BigCorp. Though, he hadn't noticed it the first two years. The desk lamp and the picture were fixed in place, so he labored to make out the leering man's features.

At St. Bonaventure's, the orphanage, Gregg underwent aptitude tests. When he grew too old, the headmaster gave him his assignment with great enthusiasm, assuring him he possessed one of the most vital jobs in the whole city. Without him, people would not get to work, commerce would not commence, and life would certainly grind to a halt. Gregg accepted the placement with a gusto reserved for only the greatest of news, and though he continued to go to his job with the same sense of duty, the gusto of his preliminary years had waned.

Three days after spotting the girl, Gregg waited at the corner. She did not show, and when he arrived to work delayed, sure enough, it held up the entire city. Humiliation filled him for having mismanaged his job. Still, Gregg fixated on the girl. Perhaps, he'd seen her on a different block. They *did* all look the same after a while.

When he walked home from work, it rained, soaking him to his soles.

At night, the sky held no stars—simply a black abyss he was too fearful to stare into because he might gaze too long and discover his true self. And who dared to know such a thing as that?

Ashamed, he did not sleep, resolved to put the girl out of his mind, and go back to his life. After all, he'd discovered how vital his job was. Without him, the train would not start. If the train did not start, the city would not go.

Gregg kept to this ethic for weeks, practically forgetting about the girl.

Then, one day, while crossing the bridge, he spotted her on the other side of the street. This time, he caught a clear view—a beauty unlike anything he'd ever seen. Her short, flaxen hair had a shine that blinded him. And her dress, the same as the first time he'd seen her, was a deep and consuming, warm and electric blue.

Stopped in his tracks, his stomach clenched and turned. A pulse ran through him. For the first time, he'd seen a sunny day, and he felt good.

She disappeared in the crowd.

At midday, while he ate lunch, the red bulb blared on, screaming across the room and illuminating Jason Big's horrific features. The whites of his eyes and the toothy smile made him cold in the rosy light.

Gregg scrambled to push his lunch out of the way and pressed the button.

His office silenced itself back into shadow.

The light pounded on again, and he pressed the button.

And when it shouted at him a third time, he held the button down with aggravated force, and it did not illuminate again for the rest of the day.

Gregg Ryan walked home that night feeling that he *did*, in fact, matter. Although his function in life was simple, it did not take away from his importance. He smiled the whole way home, the sensation of finding his sunny day lingering with him.

During dinner, he tuned into the news, whose top story was about the SkyTram.

Gregg straightened on his stool.

Earlier, around midday, a woman slipped and fell on the tracks. Sensors stopped the train for safety precautions. But right as the people on the boardwalk attempted to help her back up, the train started up again, and the woman was trapped under its wheels.

Gregg dropped his spoon as they showed a picture of the woman. A bright-blond-haired woman with a dress as blue as the heavens.

His sunny day was gone, and he wept into his pillow.

He did not show up for work the next day, or the day after that.

The city gridlocked, no one could get to work.

On the morning of the third day, he walked to work, pressed his button, and left.

He'd torn Jason Big from the wall, walked to the bridge where he'd seen the girl, smashed the awful picture, and tossed it over the side.

Light poured over Gregg.

He welcomed the sun and sky as they broke through the clouds.

Colors popped and sang. Greens and pinks and oranges. Reds and purples and…yes, blues, all came alive in the sunlight.

Gregg saw the world for the first time. He'd gazed into the void and discovered his true self. Laughing with tears in his eyes, he ran through the streets.

The train has run perpetually ever since.

II.

In every land upon the globe, legends of beasts are told, creatures of impossible quiddity, monsters of prodigious and unimaginable lore. Green Valley is no different. Some might say the valley is the source from which all manner of miraculous and mythological folk originate.

And where better for such a place to exist than in the thick woods of the great Arbor Sanctuary. The roads that cut through them are carved into the dense trees they pass. Branches weave like wicker in long tunnels connecting one town to another.

It is easy to get lost in the Arbor Sanctuary, which is probably why our poor Jinx Jenkins spent so much time there. Away from the prying eyes of the public, the judging noses and bitter whispers, Jinx retreated from the SkyTram and found refuge among the finest garden in Mother Nature's creation.

There, he slept with not a soul to vex him, nor creature to impede his sleep. Save one.

YA'HOOTIE

He's as tall as a Grizzly and twice as vicious. His hands have razors instead of nails, and his fangs are the sharpest in the animal kingdom. That's right boys, I'm talking about Ya'hootie! The Great American Ape. He's as dangerous a beast as you'll ever come across. Rip a man's arms off in a single tug. He's a ravenous monster that eats only the bloodiest of meat, howling into the night, his eyes glowing in the dark. Farmers and other people of Green Valley have reported seeing him as far back as the first settlers. Old Man Copperpot has caught him raiding his chicken coup on multiple occasions. Heck, I even saw him once late, on a night very much like this, driving home through this very Arbor Sanctuary. Damn near hit him. Just crossed the road, staring right at me and snarling with his giant teeth and psychotic eyes." Troop Master Dodson repeated the story to his Wilderness scouts over the years. Every time he told it, the beast became larger, and his performance all the more dramatic.

In a circle around the mysterious flames of the rippling campfire, Troop 1383 sat on a downed log, wrapped in their standard issue blankets, huddling close. Many of the boys had heard the tale, an infamous piece of folklore traveling well from generation to generation. And while many of the boys claimed not to be afraid of such obvious nonsense in the safety of their homes, it was another matter entirely when in the supposed domain of the beast. And at night no less. All would sleep sourly that night, letting their ten-year-old imaginations get the best of them.

All but one.

"How do they know he's as big as they say he is?" Troop 1383's newest addition, Pierre Abbé grew up in the city and had forgone the legend.

"Well, I just said, I saw him with my own two eyes," said the Troop Master.

"Right, but is there any hard evidence that proves his existence?"

"The footprints." Pierre's cousin, Tig, squawked. Tig was the youngest member of the troop, but he'd heard the story so many times, he might have told it himself. A story that would haunt him for years after his mother finished her tuck-in and kiss goodnight. "They took molds of them and everything."

"That's right, Tig. They've got them on display at the Cultural Center in Pine Bluff. Now, as I was saying, there I was in my car on my way home—"

"I get that. But if he can tear a man's arms off in one pull, is there anyone that it's happened to? And what about his age? If he's been around since the settlers, he's got to be nearly three hundred years old. I mean now, we're talking about magic." Consumed by judgment, Pierre squirmed on the log.

"Pierre. Seriously? I'm trying to tell a story. You're ruining it for the other scouts." The inquisitive addiction to the troop clearly perturbed Dodson. Not only did Pierre question everything the man said, but he'd risen to the level of Sixth Degree Wilderness scout quicker than anybody in the history of the organization. A fact the other boys refused to overlook. While it took them years to achieve such lofty heights, Pierre had simply sat down with the manual one weekend, reading it from cover to cover and performing all of the necessary tasks.

"Sorry."

The Troop Master told his stories as the boys charred marshmallows and sausages beyond recognition, eating them with smiles. Pierre sat at the end of the log, listening with feigned humor.

A year earlier Pierre's father, Tomàs, was diagnosed with an aggressive cancer on the boy's birthday. Before he turned ten, his father passed, leaving his mother and Pierre alone in the city. Christina Abbé, Pierre's mother, took her son to her family's lake house where they could be close to cousins and aunts. The uncles stayed behind, busy at their jobs, coming in occasionally for the weekends. Most of the cousins were girls, preoccupied with their dolls or domestic games. Pierre had nothing in common with them and found it less uncomfortable if he disassociated from them all together. Yet Tig, the sole male cousin in attendance and two years Pierre's junior, found revelation in the presence of another young male.

"If I have to be the groom in another one of their weddings, I might puke," he'd said as he greeted his older cousin on the rustic porch. "You wanna do Wilderness scouts with me this summer? It's a lot of fun. We go hiking and fishing and all sorts of boy stuff."

Pierre reluctantly said yes, regretting his decision the moment he put on the khaki and navy-blue uniform with the red sash and beret. "I look like the poster child for *Clean Living Magazine*."

"I don't know what that means, but it feels official. Like you're a part of something."

"The Hitler Youth comes to mind."

Tig scrunched his nose, unfamiliar with the reference.

Meanwhile, back at the annual Wilderness Jamboree, Pierre stewed over the many fallacies in the Ya'hootie story. So much that he'd let his marshmallow catch ablaze, and it was about to melt right off the stick. *Pierre watch out!*

As the sugary glob fell into the fire, he snapped back, watching it fuse with a blackened log. "Dang it."

"No worries, P. Here's another." Tig handed him a soft, white, sugar cylinder. "Do it right above the flame where it won't catch fire. I wish there was a patch for roasting marshmallows. I'd be a master class."

Pierre was more attentive this time. "Tig, if I wanted to see the Ya'hootie, is there somewhere in particular I should go?"

"What, are you crazy?"

"Say I was. Where would I go?"

"Supposedly, there's a lair up high in the sanctuary. Near the top of a mountain. They call it The Devil's Outhouse. I think 'cause it smells so bad." The little boy squinted as he remembered the details.

"Where's that?"

"Why? You're not going up there. You know we're not allowed to leave camp."

"Where is it, Tig?"

He pointed up at the shadowed ridge of the mountain line visible in the moonlight. "See that notch near the top? They call that Henderson's Knot. If you were to keep heading toward that, it would take you right there. But you're not going, P. It's too late to be walking around the woods."

"*Of course*. Just wanna know where *not* to go."

"Oh, right. Good thinking."

The boys finished eating their campfire treats and retired into their two-man pop tents. After the long hike to the camp, the troop fell quickly asleep.

All except Pierre. He lay awake, listening to the snoring boys mix with the chirping crickets and creaking trees. When he was sure it was safe, Pierre gathered up his canteen, a compass, a lantern, and the camera his father gave him for his last birthday and set out toward Henderson's Knot, dead set on proving the tale a hoax.

Climbing through brush, over stumps, naked trees, and the thick layer of dead leaves, he held his lantern in one hand and his camera in the other; something rustled behind him.

Is it him? Is it Ya'hootie?

He readied his camera and exploded a flash into the dark and screamed. A figure appeared in the burst of light.

Tig cried, falling to the ground in a fetal position.

"Tig? Why are you following me?"

"Jesus, P. I thought you were him. You shouldn't be out here." He brushed the leaves off of his uniform.

"There is no *him*. I'm gonna prove it."

"Then, I'm coming with you. Ya'hootie or not, it's not safe out here by yourself. Besides, I know where we need to go. I've been to more Jamborees than all the other scouts combined. You're already headed in the wrong direction." He grabbed the compass and held it up to the lantern.

"Fine. But Tig, you better not take me back to camp. I'm gonna prove this thing doesn't exist. It's important."

Tig held up three fingers. "Scout's honor."

The boys climbed deeper into the forest. With each step, they grew more and more isolated amongst the tall birch and pine. Clawing branches and thorny bushes scraped at their legs as elevation and night chilled their skin, all the more pronounced with every thwack and scratch. Nevertheless, Pierre trudged on, determined to prove the tale false. Childish things upset him once his father died. He refused to have anyone engaged in such a fantasy tell him that he was the unreasonable one. That he was wrong.

"The story simply had too many holes," he told Tig.

They scooted across a log bridging a ravine, the bark scratching their thighs.

"I don't care what you say, P. He's real. Master Dodson's seen him."

"Tig, I know you're young. But nothing lives forever. How could this thing be alive for hundreds of years?"

Tig adjusted his sash while collecting his dogma. "I've actually thought about that a lot. I think there might be more than one of them."

"You think, or you know?"

"All I know is they took a mold of his footprint, and based on its size, they estimated his height to be around ten feet tall." He scurried his little legs to catch up. "What I don't get is why you want to prove he doesn't exist? Everybody knows he exists. Why don't you?"

Pierre paused, his cousin running into him from behind. "Ah, just the way everybody knows Santa Clause exists, or super heroes, or ghosts."

He thought of his father.

"I just don't, okay?"

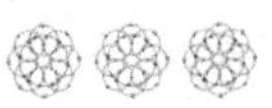

Earlier that summer, Pierre played hide-and-go-seek with the girls and Tig. He'd considered it a childish endeavor, but his mother was insistent he put down his book—what was it again…oh yes, *To Kill A Mockingbird*—and be a child for once. That meant getting out of the house, scuffing his knees, and allowing her to converse with her sisters as adults.

Begrudgingly, he left her alone, knowing his aunts conspired to set his mother up on blind dates. It didn't take an Albright Scholar to figure that out. So, he forged onward to the outside, book in hand. When the girls told him to hide, he walked away at a reasonable pace, listening to them count down from fifty.

Pierre wandered the vast yard, which stretched all the way to the tiny Lake Avalon, fed by the Élan River. He found himself in the garden of the grounds next door. It was full of winding flowerbeds, brightly-colored flora and topiary resembling various mythical beasts. Right behind the massive house was a tiny cottage, the perfect spot to hide and read his book.

He undid the latch holding the door and found a crowded room with just enough nook and a little bit of cranny to wedge himself in and read his story. But soon enough, the large, covered object taking up the space caught his attention, and he was unable to concentrate. Pierre pulled the dusty sheet to reveal a run-down Model T. It probably sat in that spot since the day it was made. He crawled inside, resting on the tattered seat cushion. Much better than the nook and far superior than any cranny.

Pierre spent the whole afternoon in the weathered jalopy, reading and enjoying his privacy. That was, until the owner of said jalopy came looking for his gardening shears.

"That's a mighty fine book you got there." The old man had a potbelly, thick silver hair, and enormous glasses. "Who might you be?"

"My name is Pierre Abbé, sir. Please, forgive me. I was simply hiding from my cousins. I didn't mean to intrude." Pierre sat up and climbed out of the ancient car.

"Ah, a little Hide 'n Seek, huh?"

"Precisely, sir. A juvenile game if I do say so myself. Yet, I found it would provide me the requisite time to engage in my book." Pierre always endeavored to give his best impression when meeting a new adult.

"Requisite? How old are you son?" he said with a hint of a laugh.

"Ten, sir. Eleven in March."

"Well, Pierre, you're a very well-spoken young man. My name is George. George Powell. I'm a professor at Ivy Pines. I was just coming out here to do some gardening to keep busy. Anything to get Martha off my back."

"Nice to make your acquaintance."

"The pleasure is all mine." He glanced back at the house for a second and hung up his shears again. "Hey, what'd you say we find you someplace a bit more comfortable to hide?"

"I must warn you, I've been brought up in the city. I'm not afraid to bite and have quite a magnificent scream." He sized up the man. "Though, had you wanted to harm me, you would have done so by now. What'd you have in mind?"

"We can go to my study. It's got better light and plenty more books."

"Lead the way."

Pierre followed George through the garden to the back-cobblestone porch and into the main house. Like his family's cabin, it, too, was expansive and finely furnished. George led him up the stairs to a room with bright windows and an entire wall of books. A rolltop desk rested in the corner alongside two plush armchairs separated by a table and lamp.

Drawn to the wall of books, Pierre took his time reading each of the titles. "A professor of what, if you don't mind me asking?"

"Folklore mostly. Of course, my true passion is cryptozoology. But no one teaches classes in that."

Pierre pulled out a thick spined book entitled *Monsters, Myths, and Legends: A Guide to the Urban Traditions of Green Valley* by George Q. Powell. He opened the book, leafing through its pages. "You don't actually believe in these things, do you?"

"On the contrary. I've devoted my life to proving the tall tales of Green Valley false. I've been out in the field and clocked countless hours of data to back myself up. I believe that it is the need to make sense of what people can't otherwise explain that causes them to latch onto such beliefs. If I can simply provide a bit of scientific proof to convince them otherwise, then I may be able to bring these simpletons into the twenty-first century. Monsters are manifestations of our fear, nothing more."

Pierre smiled at George. He'd found a like-minded colleague. And better yet, a friend.

"I just don't, Tig. Monsters are manifestations of our fear, nothing more." The boys stood in opposition, judging each other in the dim light of the lantern. Nature acted within a general rhyme and reason. If he believed the legend, he would be buying into a giant hairy man roaming the valley. That, of course, was followed by all things that should not be discussed, being classified as so-called unpopular beliefs. Maybe ghost stories were true, and super heroes, too. Was magic real, or even Santa Claus? Pierre was too logical to believe in such nonsense. And on this pretense, he set out to substantiate the legend a fraud.

"I guess." Tig hung his head, crestfallen. His tiny shoulders slumped.

Echoing through the sleepy trees came the howl of an unknown creature.

And as quick as Tig's spirits sank, he popped back up with glowing elation. "It's him."

In the deep of the Arbor Sanctuary stretching from Evergreen near the valley floor all the way to the location of the Jamboree in Pine Top, Pierre and Tig followed the sad howl, ignoring the scratching branches and sharp thorns. Young Pierre called back, cupping his hands to his face, bellowing into the night.

Ooowwwooohhh.

Tig joined in.

A yowl boomed again, much closer this time, and Tig took off running toward it, Pierre in tow. "I told you he was real. I told you."

Steps shuttered behind them, breaking branches and shuffling leaves. Pierre readied his camera with the flash on standby and raised his lantern to discover the Great American Ape; proving definitively Nature herself follows no rhyme, nor reason.

Among the no-see-ums and the pines dry with the coming autumn, among the departed vegetation of the most torpid bronze, Pierre Abbé came face to face with a beast no larger than a young child, such as himself. It stared at them, upright, with large saucer eyes, behind a snout much like that of a swine. Its hair was a long shaggy white, matted with leaves and soil. When Pierre flashed his camera, the thing's ears, pointy like a horse, perked up, its pupils swelled, and let out a stupefied squawk.

In the dry death of the forest, which rotted the leaves slowly and gave them an unbearably pungent smell, the Ya'hootie possessed a wound in its paw. For an instant, in the murmur of the napping wood, no matter what Pierre said before, there he stood, the Pygmy Bigfoot. Certainly, it was solely due to his calm and inquisitive disposition that they managed to keep their heads and not lose their wits.

Though he did not dare to show it, Pierre's blood pumped like a newly discovered oil well. For not since the discovery of the long-extinct dinosaur has one captured such a unique specimen of Nature's aloofness. Therefore, rubbing his eyes, assuring himself it was not in fact a dream, Pierre gathered his acumen and addressed the beast. With an authority not even his troop master would have believed, he said, "You are Ya'hootie."

At hearing this, the great ape broke wind, raised a leg, and wafted the stale air in the direction of the boy. Pierre—being the child he was—let out an audible giggle as his eyes watered from the sordid stench.

"He farted." Tig laughed, though the beast didn't appear to find the humor in this.

Like any Wilderness Scout worth his mettle, the boys conversed with the humanoid, gathering data about him through the bits of language it still remembered. His race was slowly being eradicated. Few beastly examples remained of his mutated species, which were it not for the overt dangers of the overreaching necessity of urban sprawl, would be a fertile and homogenous race. All were animals of chance, and the punch line to one of Mother Nature's more elaborate jokes.

Pierre later informed the *Valley Gazette* that the beast was once a settler traveling West. The settler became mysteriously ill and was abandoned in the woods, away from the wagon train, where he slept for a hundred years. All the while his body changed, evolving into the shaggy midget eventually known as Ya'hootie. When he awoke, he'd been confused and afraid, having transformed. No longer a man, he was now an abomination of one of Nature's grander perversions. He lived in the woods, alone for fifty years, cautious of the deathly lights and preoccupied valley people.

Of all the dangers the world offered, Pierre found by eliminating sickness, the pollution of its water sources, the depletion of Nature's supermarket, and other wild beasts on the hunt, the greatest menace for the few remaining Great American Ape were the encroaching valley peoples. A threat that engulfed them every day during the morning commute. Though wholly unaware of their intrusion, they depleted the beast's natural ecosystem with each new prefabricated suburban home. So with no other hill to hide upon, the ape was forced to retreat ever deeper into the diminishing tree sanctuary where the opportunistic boys were to unearth him. As a strategic defense, Ya'hootie lived deep within the Earth, in a type of den. Fearful of the society in the towns below, it grazed on berries and fish, and various types of verdant greenery.

As the race was born of an unnatural means and took quite long to gestate, few young apes existed. On the rare occasion such a beast was produced, it enjoys a short and kindly life before the grips of Nature extinguishes it from existence. Even the language the Ya'hootie remembered was minimal and base, consisting of the most fundamental of phrases and sounds. The Ya'hootie had limited use for names and referred to things by mime or tiny indeterminate squawks. Clearly a gene-memory, he prayed to the spirit of the forest, his mother, allowing every tree to embody his god. A standard ceremony consisted of dancing around the base of a tree, pounding on it with whacking palms, and howling into the night.

As the boys befriended the shaggy ape, the dawn drew closer, and the knowledge that their omitted presence would soon be noticed crept up on them. Having his proof, albeit the opposite of what he'd set out for, Pierre knew he would make George proud. Checking his camera, the picture came out quite clear. The boy's snapshot would soon be printed in the *Valley Gazette*: A portrait without pretense or decree, yet just so, in the manner of candid truth only an untrained boy of ten can take. Revealed swimming in his wooly fur, from his elongated snout down to his large feet that were grossly disproportionate, his eyes were wide with the shock of the camera's flash, his jaw agate in a near-partial smile. His rounded teeth, almost sapien in origin. Something about him made one think of the family pet.

"We have to go, Tig. The sun's coming up."

"Can we keep him?" Tig asked, unaware of how offensive a statement he'd made.

"The picture should be enough." Pierre packed away his camera as the horrors of the forest faded, the light seeping over the ridge of the mountain. If they were to expose his whereabouts to the world, it would spell certain doom for the tiny, shaggy ape. He would have to stay behind. "Besides, he's not housebroken."

"We can't leave him here. He's been alone for so long."

"Tig, on the contrary. He said it himself, he's afraid of the people below."

"Then, why isn't he afraid of us?"

Tig had a point.

"Perhaps he doesn't see us as a threat due to our age. Whatever the reason, we have to go."

Heartbroken, Tig said goodbye, giving the beast slightly larger than himself a hug. The boys headed back to camp, elated over their new discovery. When they returned, Dodson was not yet awake, so the boys, surreptitious to the rest of the troop, settled back in their tents and caught a few remaining hours of needed sleep.

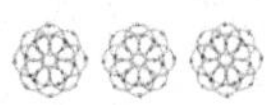

All along the Élan river, deep ravines carved out the landscape, creating an intricate system of bridges. The ravines were the product of glaciers carving the land during the last ice age. They became the dried-up tributaries to the river flowing with run off from the valley mountains in the rainy spring months. By summer, they were a conglomerated mess of mud and leaves and creepy-crawly things. Many mothers believed the mud itself, and the prospect of laying havoc to their freshly cleaned homes, drew boys to the ravines in the first place.

Pierre and Tig were no exception. It was, in fact, in those ravines, with dirt under his nails and muck in his shoes, that Pierre rediscovered what it was to be a boy. Soon, he left his books behind and used his imagination, playing with Tig in the reverberating ravines under the bridges and howling under the sun.

On one such day, the boys found themselves reunited with their furry friend from the mountain. Despite his instinctual fears of the townspeople and urban encroachment, the petite primate was all the more intrigued by his encounter with the two boys. He sought the boys using his swine-like snout, happening upon them in the middle of a game of Treasure Hunters.

Back when he'd first met the boys, he felt a reminiscence toward Pierre lingering deep within his DNA. The rare beast held up its hand, exposing a cleanly naked palm, hoary and Caucasian. Across the lifeline fold was a gash he'd acquired after inspecting the blades of the creature that ate the trees. Systematically, Pierre took note of the tiny paw, a doppelganger of his own.

The Pygmy Bigfoot grinned, his teeth porcelain and square in the moonlight. The rarest of all beasts was relishing the indescribable consolation of still having a soul. Something he was sure he'd lost in the woods many years ago. He had the sudden instinct to make a fire and tell a story. Perhaps, even paint something on a wall in his den.

It was something in the Ya'hootie that came from his very genetic makeup, that which is known as empathy or admiration for the little boys. For he knew of what terrible and horrific things life had yet to thrust upon them. If he merely remembered how to speak the words, it would have made the poor boys feel an all-consuming love. A love which might have lessened if the beast had shared he similarly admired Pierre's canteen and compass. And *had* the boy been told, he would have become shrunken by his dissatisfaction. For what man can ever truly find satisfaction by what is so easily given? But rightly so, the empathy and admiration were true from Ya'hootie, since with a thing so futile could not be tapered in the heart of a beast.

An old misnomer exists about the word *empathy*. That it is something learned through stories or religion or the teachings of elders. And if empathy is learned, it must only be in the hearts of man, rather than an inherent function of all living things, regardless of kingdom, class, order, genus, or species. Yet, in the dryness of the dark forest, no interpretation exists of one's empathy or admiration. Simply the feeling itself is enough. Empathy is to know one's self through the vision of another. Empathy is to know the whole history of a boy before he is grown. Empathy is to know the pain of others as your own. Empathy is to smile out of empathy. Ya'hootie blinked, smiling into Pierre's lantern—kind, hairy, true, and kind.

For this reason, Ya'hootie scoured the mountainside, trekked into town, and hid under bridges. Until finally, he reunited with the two boys from the valley crag.

"*Ya'hootie*." The delight in Tig's scream made the peaceful beast beam once more, knowing they remembered him.

"You shouldn't be here." Pierre hurried over to him. "It's not safe."

Ya'hootie told them that he loved them, too.

The boys decided to hide their unusual acquaintance under a bridge near their family's cabin.

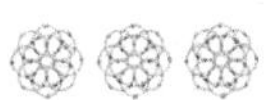

At nightfall, they hurried out under the cover of darkness and tucked the beast in George's shed with the Model T, leaving him some leftovers from dinner. As ecstatic as they were to have their friend back, Pierre's sense of responsibility came crashing home, keeping him from sleeping. He needed to show George. It was the only logical thing to do.

The next morning when Pierre tumbled out of bed, he rushed over to the shed, his camera in tow, to take stock of Ya'hootie's well-being. The minute man was fine. And though Pierre couldn't put his finger on it, his friend seemed changed. Perhaps, it was his snout—maybe it appeared smaller; or his fur—free of knots and groomed; or maybe simply his general disposition—placidly pleasant. Whatever the change, something was altered.

When Pierre asked him if he enjoyed his accommodations, the ape replied in the affirmative, having taken a special liking to the ancient automobile and its soft seats. Better than a pile of leaves, he told Pierre. Something about having successfully cared for someone else made Pierre's heart swell.

But the hard part was still to come. He must tell George. If anyone knew what to do, it would be him. Pierre left Ya'hootie in the shed and made his way up to the old man's house where George and his wife, Martha, enjoyed their morning coffee.

"So, Mr. Abbé, how was your excursion into the Arbor Sanctuary?" George said through his bristly mustache.

"Quite eventful. In fact, I have a situation of great note I simply must show you, sir." Pierre noted Martha's smile, and though she was a kindly woman, he did not wish to involve more people than necessary.

George understood, and they retreated to his study, as they'd grown accustomed to do over the course of that summer.

"Well, my boy, what do you have for me?"

Pierre handed the camera over, and George looked at the candid photo.

"That's *some* costume you boys made up there. Is this Tig? Quite lifelike."

"It's not Tig, sir. It's the genuine article. That is Ya'hootie." George narrowed his brow, and Pierre relayed the events of their nighttime march.

"Normally, I would play along with a boy your age, but because you are unlike other boys, Pierre, I hope you will understand my skepticism. I have dedicated my entire life's work to proving such a beast a fallacy. Without hard evidence that this photo is authentic, I'm afraid I'll have to hold true to my doubts."

"Naturally, I expected you to say that. In any other set of circumstances, I would side with you as a cynic, but I assure you, what I have told you is the truth. My proof is in the shed. I hope you do not mind, but he slept in the Model T. He's waiting there now." Pierre pointed out the window.

When any person adamantly denies the existence of a thing, it is because, quite often, he wishes for nothing more than to be proven wrong. As the bard said, *Me thinks doth protest too much.* So it was for the old man, when he hurried to the glass pain of the study, and through the window of the shed, two large saucer eyes peered up at him.

George's face paled like a specter. "That's not possible."

"I assure you, sir, it is. And I only tell you now, because I knew you, of all people, would know what to do."

Without looking at the boy, George spoke in a daze, steadying himself on a chair. "Is he safe? Are there others? How did you get him back here? I have so many questions."

"All will be answered if you would kindly accompany me to the shed. I'm sure he'll be more than forward when providing answers."

"He speaks?"

"In a way, yes. Now, sir, please. He is waiting."

Pierre led his flabbergasted mentor to the shed where Ya'hootie customarily greeted him with a fart. As the day grew long, Ya'hootie and Pierre recanted the small simian's history to George. With every supplementary detail, the man sunk more and more into the giddiness of a child. He must have waited for this all his life, although likely afraid to admit it to himself, he'd wanted the stories to be true maybe more than anyone.

Pleased with himself, Pierre made the right decision.

"I need to write a book. This is simply too big to pass up."

"But if we expose him, he'll never be safe." The boy hurried to Ya'hootie's side.

That shook the man from his fantasies of literary and professional acclaim. "Well, yes. There is that. Perhaps, we could take him to the zoo?"

"And keep him in a cage—I think not, sir. He has known no other life but that of freedom. He must be allowed to roam in his natural habitat. We have to take him back to the Sanctuary. It's where he belongs."

"Yes, of course. You surprise me at just how adult you really are, my boy. A cage would never do. But, let me study him. I'll write my book, then we will release him. After all, you don't wish to say goodbye to him just yet. You have quite the rapport with the little guy."

Pierre could not argue. He'd found a friend in the woods that night. A friend he was not yet ready to give up. So, it was settled. Ya'hootie would say for a little while longer.

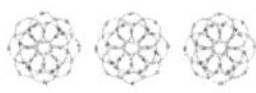

Christina Abbé, Pierre's mother, had been in and out of relationships since the age of fourteen. In high school, it seemed she'd gone out with a new boy every week. Although not quite that dramatic, she dated boys for as long as it took her to grow bored with them. For some, it was a few months, others the course of a weekend. But she never let herself be single for more than a few days.

In college, at Ivy Pines, she was in a long-distance relationship for her first semester, sure of herself this was *the one*. But soon enough, she went to parties, and her pace from high school quickened. She stayed with young men as long as it took them to finish in bed. In her sorority, she even experimented with a few sisters, but never deemed it more than a mild fascination.

Her manic love life came to a resounding halt when she met Tomàs Abbé, a foreign student, and fell madly in love with him. They dated a few years until they both graduated and married quickly thereafter. Following their wedding night, nine months later, they had Pierre, and her life appeared perfect for a time.

When Tomàs was diagnosed with an aggressive cancer, and by the time Pierre turned ten, his father passed. Now, alone for the first time in her life, Christina was feeling that old itch again. The only difference was that she now felt guilty about it. She couldn't place why.

While her son was away during the summer days, her sisters meddled round the clock in setting her up with men from around the valley. Christina knew Pierre wanted nothing more than for her to learn about herself, and discover who she was, and what she wanted, without a man. She always adapted to the men in her life, including Tomàs, giving their son a French name instead of her deceased father's, and never truly knowing her own unique identity.

The suitors included a cast of characters distinct in their own way. Yet, Pierre and Tig had a furry trump card up their sleeve and refused to let any of them sink their hooks in his mother.

Thor, the bodybuilding accountant, had a shaved head which blinded those he talked to with its reflection from the sun. Thor received a thumbtack on the doorbell.

Jerry, the news anchor, was so tan he glowed like a red bulb. He drove a Corvette, which resembled his unfortunate pigment. Jerry got a clogged tailpipe and a chewed-up transmission—all Ya'hootie's idea.

Michael, the morbidly obese faith healer, convinced Christina to give him a massage to aide his failing body. When she left the room to procure some oil, the boys sent in the tiny ape. Ya'hootie dug his fingers into Michael's doughy tissue. When the enormous man complained, he twisted around to find the beast's patented freakish smile. Michael fled the house in a mere towel.

The owner of the local video rental store, Mort, had gone to high school with Christina and was one of the few boys she'd passed up. Mort hadn't aged well, developing a ring of hair and a goofy mustache, taking up residence in the apartment above his mother's garage. Yet, Christina grew seemingly desperate and agreed to join him for a nightcap in his tiny abode. When Mort kissed Christina, the boys unleashed Ya'hootie's utilitarian passing of wind. When the fetid stink reached Mort's nose, he choked for air. Christina was never asked back.

With Pierre unable to protect his mother at all times, she soon began a relationship with Steven Some, the owner of a pet store in Avalon. He was a boisterous and indignant man, who held little affection toward children but a fondness for Christina's curves. They saw one another regularly as she left Pierre to attend to his childhood.

The first encounter Pierre had with Steve was when Christina took her son to the pet store, which was dark and smelled of foul rancorous things. Glass aquariums and mesh cages holding all assortments of canines, felines, rodentia, reptile, and chordata crammed along the walls. In the center, large wired cages contained parrots, canaries, finches, and cockatiels. Though the store was virtually empty of patrons, a constant buzz filled the room from the various prisons. The animals squirming and fidgeting and slithering in captivity sickened Pierre's stomach. He made for the door when Christina cut him off and introduced him to the infamous Steve.

"Pierre, say hello to Mr. Some," she said.

The boy extended his hand, suppressing queasy nausea. Balding with stringy hair that hung long in back, Steve's face wore a large doorknob of a nose and dark sunken eyes. He smiled at the boy, sure Christina regarded his effort, never making eye contact with Pierre.

"Hey there, little buddy. I'm Steve. How d'you like my store? Do you like animals?" He nodded his head at the boy as if answering for him.

When Pierre did his best to answer, a flood of sick beset Steve's crotch like a mortar.

"Aw, son of a—Christina, these are Egyptian cotton. For Christ's sake." He hurried behind the counter and sopped up the mess. "Some kid you got there. A real charmer."

Christina lowered her eyes and rushed to help.

Pierre recognized something in his mother he'd never before believed possible. She was meek and pitiful and pathetic—the most tragic thing he'd ever known. He loved his mother, and refused to allow such an insolent man to take her from him. Thus, he planned to rid the evil man from their lives.

Over the next few weeks, while Christina courted the vile Steve, Pierre and Ya'hootie worked industriously. Upon every encounter the man had with Pierre's mother, the boy and his stout companion sabotaged the proceedings. They filled the man's shoes with dung, assailed his car with bedbugs, put laxative in his food, and even poison ivy on his toilet paper. Nevertheless, Steve kept coming back, seeing Christina as a prize to be owned. He would not falter until he'd obtained his trophy.

And when they quite nearly gave up, Pierre hashed out one final plan. He and Ya'hootie would sneak into Steve's store at night and liberate the animals from their incarceration. Ya'hootie was especially excited, as he found the imprisonment of defenseless animals abhorrent.

It was against every fiber in his being.

It had to be done.

Meanwhile, as George charted and recorded his findings on the Great American Ape, Pierre detected a continued change in his fuzzy friend. The transformation was unmistakable. Ya'hootie shed his fur in clumps, leaving a mess about the shed. His ears, so horse-like before, shrank to something of a pointy-eared elf. The eyes, which were once like dark reflecting glasses, also became more hominid with distinct irises and pupils. No change was more apparent than that of Ya'hootie's feet. The large clodhoppers he'd become so famous for were down to the manageable girth of a men's size-fourteen sneaker.

"It pains me to say it, my boy, but I believe our friend has over stayed his biological welcome. We need to take him back before it gets too late," George said one day in his study.

"We can't. I need him." Pierre's voice panicked, full of fear.

"P, I love him, too, but he's sick." Tig pulled at his cousin's sleeve.

"Hear me out. Without him, my mother might end up with this nincompoop for the rest of her life. Like I said, I *need* him." But down deep, Pierre knew what he needed was far more than to use his downy companion as a tool. He was not ready to let him go. For in the few weeks he'd know Ya'hootie, he'd come to love him in a way he'd not felt since his father died. The idea of abandoning the tiny man in the woods was too much to bear. Ya'hootie thawed a place in Pierre's heart that had long gone cold. And when he considered the beast's absence, it was all he could do to hold back the chill of tears.

George read the boy's face and placed a hand on his tiny shoulder. "Pierre, have I ever told you the story of the Model T?"

"No, sir. I was waiting for you to say something. I didn't want to intrude."

"My father built them in his youth. Worked in the Ford plant for twenty years. When I was a boy, he always struggled to get me to help him out in our garage, but I was determined to be more than a mechanic. But my son, Charlie, he *loved* cars. He learned to work on them in high school and got a job in a garage when he graduated. Being a professor, I felt this was below him. He was smart. Not as smart as you, but smart all the same. We fought over the prospects of his future, me always pushing for him to get his degree. When Charlie was twenty-two, he enlisted and was sent overseas. Suddenly, everything we fought over seemed so petty. I got him that car from a junkyard as a going away present. I promised him that when he came back we'd work on it together. I never got that chance. He died in battle right before they pulled the troops out. After that, I couldn't bear to look at it, but giving it up was not an option. It stayed here, covered, for years, until I found you reading in it that day."

"So, that's where you were hiding," Tig said.

George smiled at Tig, who was far too young to understand the story's weight. "I kept that car in there for years, decades. All the while, it's grown more and more decrepit; falling apart and rusting through. That car is my last connection to my boy. But no matter what I do, I can't bring myself to face it. But that's a car. Not a living thing. I can't let you do the same to Ya'hootie. I won't let you do that to yourself."

Fighting through the sniffles, Pierre said, "But what about my mother?"

"That's a problem your mother will have to figure out on her own, son. We can't force the people in our lives to see what we want them to see about themselves. They have to come to it on their own terms. Have faith. She seems to be a smart lady. I think she'll come around on her own."

"And the animals? Ya'hootie said he can't leave them behind."

George looked away for a time. "Son, I'm sorry, but I can't, in good faith, allow you to commit such an egregious crime."

"But—"

"That is why we'll do it together. If we get caught, I can take the fall. I can't have you risking your future. We'll take the animals with us when we return our hairy friend."

Pierre hugged the man tight. The plan was set.

That night, the boys and George placed the metamorphosing Ya'hootie in the back of George's truck and headed into town. The sleeping metropolis put its lights out. George pulled his truck around the back of the store in the alley. The band of liberators let themselves into the shop with the keys they'd stolen that afternoon and emptied every tank into the bed of the truck.

Frightened at first, the animals calmed themselves at the sight of Ya'hootie.

They unlatched cages and scooped the fish into baggies.

They cradled the puppies and carried the out the bird cages.

The team worked through the night until every last animal was loaded, brimming with life, in the bed of George's truck.

One last cage remained, a family of hamsters, and Pierre went to retrieve it. And as he reached for the handle, a flashlight shown through the front door.

Pierre froze.

A policeman, probably making the nightly rounds, peered in at the empty store. He moved the beam of light about, catching Pierre in mid-grab.

The officer called through the glass. "Son, what do you think you're doing?"

Terrified and unsure what to do, he said the first thing that came to his head. "Going out of business. Just packing up the store."

"Sorry to hear that. Didn't realize business was down. Steve around?"

"He—uh—was—but uh—he left me, my cousin, and my grandfather to finish up."

"Need any help?"

"*No.* I mean, we're just leaving now."

"Sounds good. If you don't mind, I want to call this in. Just to be sure."

Pierre panicked. He held the hamster cage in his hand, seeing his path to freedom out the back. Suddenly, the officer's squad car lit up, sounding its sirens and shrieking its horn. Beyond the rotating lights, Ya'hootie was visible through the windshield.

"What the—" The policeman hurried back to his car.

Pierre rushed out the door and into the truck. As they rounded the corner of the alley, they snatched up Ya'hootie, accelerating out of town and into the thick of the Arbor Sanctuary. The deeper they journeyed, the more Ya'hootie's hair sprouted back, the piggier his snout became, the longer his ears stretched, and the larger his feet grew. When they came to the end of a dirt trail, they helped the Pygmy Bigfoot out of the truck and onto the familiar forest floor.

They freed the animals in waves as the prisoners found their way to the sanctuary of the great woods.

When the last cage lay empty, George shook Ya'hootie's paw, having grown a deeper appreciation for the beast, promising to never reveal its location.

Tig hugged him, full of tears, promising he'd come back and visit. Though he didn't know it then, none of them would see that great example of Nature's wit again.

Pierre strained to say goodbye, but the words wouldn't come. His throat clenched and only let out a tiny squawk.

But for Ya'hootie, it seemed enough. As he considered the boy, becoming a familiar color, a kind of orangey-blue tinge, like the sun rising at dawn, he recognized what a bright boy he must be. For the boy, he felt nothing but empathy—

you remember empathy—and admiration. Taking Pierre's hand, he placed it upon his head and gave the boy a nod.

Right as the thing fully achieved his wild state, another beast howled in the distance. *Ooowwwooohhh.* He spun on instinct and hurried off into the woods, stopping for a moment to wave and call back in his own scratchy voice, "Goodbye."

When the three explorers arrived home, George said goodnight, and they parted ways. Tig headed straight to bed, exhausted from the trip. Pierre, on the other hand, spotted the light in his mother's room. He found her alone on her bed, reading one of his books—it might have been *Ordinary People*, but who's to say.

"Mom? I thought you were out with Steven."

"I was," she said putting down the book. "We went out, and he took me to a nice restaurant. It started out as a great night, but he ruined it when he told me he needed money. He owes a man in town that was threatening to go after his business."

"You're joking. I'm sure of it."

"I know. Can't win 'em all, huh, kiddo."

"What did you do?"

"I had him bring me back early. I gave him the money and told him to never speak to me again."

"Really?" Pierre had hope for his mother for the first time.

"I think I'm going to take some time off dating. Besides, I've already got my man right here." She leaned over and kissed him on the cheek. "Enough about me. What were you and Tig up to tonight?"

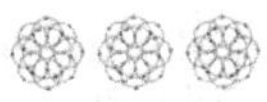

When the sun broke and spilled over the valley the next day, Pierre and Tig told George that they wanted to help him work on the Model T. At the end of summer, when they'd healed the car into working order, they road it out to the Arbor Sanctuary, hanging out the windows and howling at the moon.

Though Ya'hootie's location was never revealed, Pierre's picture of him in the *Green Valley Gazette* caught the attention of the people in Green Valley, confirming to them even the wildest of imaginations were no match for that of Mother Nature.

III.

The Great American Institution of baseball is enjoyed in all corners of the globe. And anyone who has a team to follow knows the priority of their team's shot at the title. Every waking minute spent worrying and wishing, deliberating and analyzing. For some, baseball is a kind of church, capable of teaching them all the lessons they need in this life if they merely found the patience. After all, baseball is a game of the soul. That's what Pedro Marinez says anyhow.

In Green Valley, an estimable amateur league of independent teams, dubbed the Arbor League, found asylum in the tiny hamlets and charming villages spanning the leafy vale. Early in its formation, Arthur Pimlington, founder of what later became BigCorp, helped establish the coalition, and his progeny has governed it ever since.

Of these teams, Evergreen's Evereadys were maybe the most popular, and certainly the most forlorn. A team that rose to prominence in the golden years of this country, vying for championships with regularity, and providing dramatics unknown by any of the foremost scholars of Shakespeare. Yet, as all teams do, they wore themselves out like an old mitt, sinking into the depths of melancholy and collapse.

Many attribute this fall from greatness to none other than our pathetic companion, Jinx Jenkins. For it was in the last of the Evereadys' bids for the valley championship, after gaining a sizeable lead in the standings, that they suddenly began to slump. The edge they'd made for themselves stretched like the seventh well into the playoffs, but it was not without its setbacks. That was, until Jinx was discovered taking up residence in a small space under the floorboards of the Evereadys' dugout.

After all, baseball has an otherworldly quality to it, and superstition is simply one of its many pillars.

When the vagrant was discovered, the outrage was deafening. Poor Jinx received cups of chewing-tobacco spit and beer dumped on his head, bottles thrown at his body, and curses only a mother could provide spat at him in the harshest of timbres. In the truest sense of a scapegoat, they chased him out of town, providing him with his unfortunate moniker.

The 'Readys lost the championship and have not recovered since.

THE BALLPARK POET

The day was hot in midsummer, and the season was halfway gone. The team hadn't managed a winning record since game two of the opening series. Nevertheless, by the fourth inning of that game, the fans had packed the stands. Hotdog venders, carrying their heavy metal vats, paced the aisles for some time already. With the score well out of hand, the fans grew restless for the real attraction of the afternoon.

After the third strike of the third out, the home team took the field. And that's when the fans saw him. Crumbs stuck in the corners of his bristly mustache. His bulbous paunch sagged over his beltline. The foam pad wrapped around his neck for what little comfort it offered. He started his call simple enough.

"Beer here." His words cut across the crowd.

A boy in the third row turned with a giant grin, tugging at his father's sleeve.

"If you wanna beer, *guess what,* I'm here. So don't fret, don't fear. Don't shed a tear. All life's worries can be solved with a beer." The crowd laughed.

A man stood up and said, "Yeah, but will it make this game bearable?"

The crowd laughed again.

"You ask if this game will be bearable. But I must submit, that you are hysterical. Hysterical if you cannot see clear. Of course, the game will be better with a beer."

The heckler chortled and sat down.

"Sit back, relax, there's a long way to go. Cheer for our boys, and enjoy the show."

Not only did the fans applaud, but even the players chuckled, dishing out a collective woot.

The people returned their attention to the game as the vendor made his way down aisle 124, unable to walk more than a few steps at a time as patron after thirsty patron waved him over for a piece of the action. A weathered Evergreen Evereadys hat flagged him down, the white cursive E on the front browned with sweat. The smile on the young man's face held the same anticipation reserved for the first pitch of the season.

"Hey, Mac. We'll take two Bach Lites." He motioned to the curvy woman to his left.

"Two Bach Lites, out'a sight. Drink a few more, you'll be just right. A couple more, and you might get tight. So, let's not do that." The vendor nodded at the rosy-cheeked woman. "With a girl like yours, you'll want to make it to tonight."

Mac, the vendor, gave the young man a knowing wink. The man snorted, and the woman blushed. As he took the beers, he gladly handed over a twenty-dollar bill.

"Keep the change, Mac."

"Big tipper, big tipper. Any more singles, people'll think I'm a stripper." The vendor put his hands behind his head and wiggled his hips at the crowd.

A large curly-haired woman in pink juicy-print sweatpants, rushed past the vender, nudging him so some of the water from his ice chest splashed on a fan's sandaled foot, making him cringe.

Mac put his hand on the man's shoulder to reassure him.

"Juicy, Juicy. Watch where you're going. The 'J' and the 'Y' are certainly bowing." She stopped on the steps to look at the vendor. "All you need do is say 'excuse me.' No need to cop-a-feel, batter, abuse me. Say you're sorry to this nice man, whose foot is frozen as this here can."

He held up the can he'd finished pouring from. The woman couldn't help but acknowledge his command for an apology. Her guilt kicked in, and she made her way back up to the wincing man.

She apologized and the poet touched her on the shoulder.

"I say, lady, if you want to make nice, buy this fella a beer, cold as ice."

She went to her row, conversed with her husband, and returned with a few loose dollar bills.

The vender made his way around the stands, stopping every few feet with a new and improvised jingle for each customer. The game lagged on as the summer heat sweltered. Fans laughed at his quips, almost always forking over more than required, followed by, "Keep the change." And Mac took it, stuffing the excess bills in his black fanny pack.

As he passed each row, the fans all conspired about the beer man's origins. One man told his kids that he heard the vender was an out-of-work comic, who turned to hawking beer during the recession. A row behind him, another man said that he once played for the Evereadys but was beaned in the head and hadn't said a word since that wasn't in rhyme. A few sections over, a young woman said that her father was in the Army with him. They'd fought in the war together, and he'd saved their entire platoon. He was once a poetry teacher, another man chimed in. And another said that he was a Shakespearean actor.

The truth was, nobody had a clue who he was or where he came from. When fans asked him, he always agreed with their story, in turn cultivating his myth beyond any actual truth. He figured the grander the legend became, the more beer he could sell. After all, this was a job.

His solitary tell was after each finely-crafted quip, he looked to the field to see how the most recent play turned out. When there was a strike out or an easily caught fly ball, he grimaced, as if somehow finding himself to blame. The fans that did take note assumed he was a rabid fan of the Evereadys.

Then, his eyes would perk up and target in on the next thirsty fan.

By the seventh inning on Jimmy's first day, his legs wobbled and his back ached. The ice chest was still full of beer. Nobody wanted to buy from him. They all wanted "the guy that rhymes," or "The Poet." Jimmy figured peddling beer at the ballpark was the perfect summer gig. He'd get tan, fit, and most of all, he'd get a chance to watch his beloved Evereadys.

Since a kid, Jimmy had followed them in the papers and on the radio. His father took him to a few games back when the team sat at the top of the standings. But since his father left, he hadn't been back. He'd heard rumors of the Ballpark Poet from his classmates but never thought much of it.

Every team had its sideshow attractions.

Pine Ridge had Aunt Tessa, whose booming voice blanketed the field. In Walden, a group of men played instruments out of time and rhythm. Green Creek let the fans coach the team via giant YES and NO signs for a few games each season. In Pinehurst, they had a seventh inning dance off, and Rocky Top threw a Jackalope sausage eating contest every fifth inning, curtesy of Jackalope Jerry's.

Everywhere you went, the attraction was different. And every fan believed their park was the best.

Jimmy stood in the entranceway of section 103. He put his ice chest down and rubbed his back, pulling off his father's old, hunter-green Evereadys hat and wiping the sweat from his brow.

"I wouldn't let them catch you doing that if I were you, kid." A gruff voice came from behind him.

Sol, a pruned old man with a gray mustache and squinty eyes, carried a cotton-candy tree with a few selections left. Despite his age and well-baked skin, he was in great shape. Jimmy spotted the Sailor Jerry tattoo and imagined the old man with a seamen's cap and a pipe.

"Hey, Sol. Suppose you're right. Wouldn't want to piss 'em off on my first day." He bent, hiked the strap over his shoulder, and lifted with his back.

"Jesus, kid. Didn't they teach you anything before they sent you out here? You gotta lift with your knees. You'll kill your back that way. Don't you know nothing?"

"I guess not."

Sol was the only person Jimmy knew at the park so far. He liked the old codger, reminding him of his Grampy, always huffing and puffing about something, yet always with the best of intentions.

"I'll try to remember that."

"You best memorize it, son. You won't make it through the season if you keep doing it your way. I know. This is season thirty for me. I've had about every injury you could think of on this job." Sol took off his hat and scratched his naked scalp. "Don't worry, kid. You'll get used to it. Gotta build up your strength. Doesn't happen overnight."

He slapped Jimmy on the ass and moved on.

"I gotta sell some beer is what I *gotta* do. Hey, Sol?"

The man looked back at Jimmy.

"Who is he? You been here so long, you gotta know."

Sol gazed out across the stadium, the crowd going wild for the anonymous beer vendor. "Name's Bob. But everybody calls him Mac. Don't know why. Other than that, not really sure. He's been here forty some-odd years. Nice guy. We go for a beer after the games sometimes. As for who he is, ask him. He'll give you a different story each time. Got tired of trying to figure it out myself."

Sol glanced at the seats higher up and a sparkle came to his eye. "Gotta run, kid. Think I see me a little girl with a sweet tooth in row fifty-four."

And he was off, with more pep in his step than Jimmy would achieve all day.

After the game, Sol invited Jimmy to join him and Mac for a brew at the Stealing Home Saloon across from the park. He struggled to hide his excitement at the chance to get pointers from the two veterans, especially after his day of minimal sales and even fewer tips. He accepted the offer, and after he was done cashing out with the vendor manager for the night, Jimmy headed across Pimlington Way to the saloon, which was in correspondence with Pimlington Grounds, the

Eveready's stadium, named for the prodigious Arthur Pimlington.

Inside the saloon sat a long mahogany bar on one side and green booths made of torn vinyl on the other. Black duct tape patched many of the booths in peeling strips. The sticky floor held the faintest trace of vomit that establishments of its kind had on warm summer days. Along the walls hung old black-and-white photos of Evereadys' players of days gone by. The championship team of '63 was featured on one wall, surrounded with newspaper clippings to mark the occasion. The headline read, "Evereadys plunder Pirates to Win Championship Booty." The line below it read, "Megger Evers Assassin Still At Large." A jukebox played music his mother brought him up on: soap bubble rock 'n' roll with just an innuendo of sex.

Halfway down the bar sat Mac and Sol, sipping on their sweaty tankards. They spoke to the bartender, a clean-shaven middle-aged man still sporting a crew cut from his days in the service. Stains marked his white T-shirt, and he wore thick black horn-rimmed glasses. When he looked up at Jimmy's approach, the other two men turned to greet him.

"Mac, Tom, this is the kid I was telling you about." Sol paused, struggling to recall the name.

"Jimmy," he offered, saving Sol from the strain.

"S'right. Jimmy. I don't know. For some reason, I wanted to call you Suds." His mouth opened in a toothy grin.

"You mean as in a frosty mug of beer? Hell, buy me one, and I could get behind that." Jimmy was simply happy to be invited.

Mac examined him straight-faced and serious before he gave Jimmy a smile, curling his mustache and inviting him to sit. "Kid's all right, Sol. Like him already. Sit down, I'll buy you brew."

Those were the first words Jimmy heard from the man that didn't rhyme. That rumor was trashed.

"Thanks, Mac. I didn't exactly make a whole lot in the way of beer money today."

"Aw, hell. Was I hogging all the customers again? That happens. Sorry. I get going, and sometimes, I just don't know when to stop." Mac tapped the side of his nose and gave Jimmy a wink.

"Mac, you're a real ass, you know that?" Sol slammed his glass on the bar, foam spilling over the edge.

"Hey, man, you gotta thing, and it works. Can't fault you for that." Jimmy shrugged.

"He's still an ass." Tom put the mug down in front of Jimmy. "You're twenty-one, right?"

He was scarcely eighteen.

"Yeah, course. What'd you think, I'm some kind of kid?"

The older men laughed.

"Right, kid." Tom winked and left him to it.

Other than the four of them, a few patrons sat in the back at a booth, and a couple more played pool. Aside from the dim lights at the bar, a lamp hung above the pool table, shaded by a Kromer's Beer logo, leaving the rest to darkness.

"Mac, Suds here was asking me about you earlier. Wanted to know your story." Sol coughed out a laugh.

"Yeah, what'd you tell him?"

"Told him he'd have to ask you that."

"Well, what'd ya wanna know?"

Jimmy took a giant swig from the beer, afraid that Tom was going to wise up any minute. He gulped it down and wiped the foam from his face. "What's your story? Where are you from? You have to hear the people talking about you. No one is that inept."

Mac scoffed.

"Inept? Sol, we got ourselves a regular College Joe here." He took a sip of his beer. "Yeah, I hear 'em. I've heard 'em all. One guy asked me if it was true I'd been the Ring Leader in a traveling circus."

"And?"

"And what? 'Course I was. I also fought in World War II, Korea, and Vietnam. I used to be on Broadway. I once ran for Governor. And I've even appeared in several adult movies." He leaned over to Sol. "I don't know if I mentioned this one yet. Did you know I speak twelve languages?"

Sol sat up straight. "Yeah? Name 'em."

"English, Spanish, French, Italian, Farsi, Russian, Chinese—both Mandarin and Cantonese—Japanese, Finish, and Latin."

Tom counted on his fingers. "That's eleven."

"And Sanskrit."

"That's not a fucking language." Sol chirped up.

"Screw yourself."

They roared.

Each listed the different rumors Mac had heard over the years as they got properly sauced. Before long, it was closing time.

"Boys, you don't gotta go home, but you can't stay here," said Tom as he polished a glass. They stood from their stools and exited through the swinging saloon door.

"I'll see you gentlemen. Lavern is gonna be pissed when I get home. Just remembered she cooked pot roast tonight." Buzzed, Sol's face pinched.

"Is that the roast that tastes like a wet dog?" Mac jabbed the old man's ribs.

"That's the one. I'm off."

Mac lit a cigarette and offered one to Jimmy. He accepted, even though he wasn't a smoker. "So what's the truth?"

"Jesus, kid, you don't let up. You don't get it do you? They're all true."

"What do you mean they're all true? That's impossible."

"They're all true because people want them to be true. The myth is more interesting, so I let 'em believe what they want. It took me a while, but I realized these fans are marks. They came for a show. They want to be entertained. Baseball's only part of it. If all they wanted was the game, they could sit at home and listen to the radio. We gotta give 'em more. What'd ya think they've got the bat spin races and that idiot dressed up like a pine tree out there for? It's all a show, kid. I'm simply an attraction."

Jimmy's insides clenched as he gagged on the cigarette, spitting out smoke. "At this point, you're the main attraction. I bet half our errors are on account of you distracting the players."

"Only half?" He snorted, looking at the sidewalk in silence. "See you tomorrow, Suds."

Mac flicked his cigarette to the wall, and the ashes exploded. He walked down Pimlington Way and turned the corner, out of sight.

Realizing that he didn't smoke, Jimmy flicked the cigarette in the same manner as Mac but failed as it flew half way and plummeted to the sidewalk. Should he follow Mac to see where such a legend lived? Maybe, it would shed some insight on who he was. He held onto the idea for a minute before deciding it was creepy.

After a minute more, his curiosity caught the best of him. Jimmy chased down the avenue to find him. Yet, despite the well-lit motorway, Mac had disappeared.

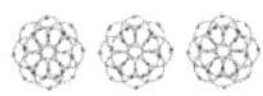

That night, when Jimmy returned home, the lights were off, his mother long asleep. Dinner waited for him on the kitchen counter, wrapped in tin foil. He took his food upstairs, setting it on the dresser next to his bed. His room was tiny, and although he was a budding adult, posters from his childhood choked the wall space. Humphrey Bogart scowled from a poster for a detective movie, and an Eveready's player from his youth, Dusty "Corncob" Ellison posed in another. In the corner hung a tall full-length mirror, and Jimmy walked over to it, ignoring his dinner.

He slouched his awkward frame, popping out his volleyball belly, and strained to imagine what he'd look like with a dusty-blonde mustache.

"It's all a show, kid. I'm simply an attraction." He mimicked the weathered baritone of Mac's voice. "If you're wife's a bitching, get out of the kitchen. If you're bored to death, don't hold your breath. 'Cause the Evereadys are terrible, and it's just not bearable. But my friends, no need to fear. I have a tub full of beer. So shut your traps, get your eye on the prize. Why not try a Bach Lite on for size?"

He shook his head. Not quite as good as Mac, but not half-bad.

He squinted at himself and said, "Suds. I like it."

Over the next few weeks, Jimmy sat at the bar after every game with Mac and Sol, shooting the bull, reminiscing about teams of old, players of yesteryear. Jimmy impressed the men with his vast knowledge of the sport. He learned early on that baseball fans test each other's merit through anecdotes and statistics. The men threw up a name, and Jimmy finished their quiz with a batting average or famous play.

His fascination with Mac's true origins never faltered. Every night, he secretly followed the man down the street, skulking in the shadows. But at some point, Jimmy'd lose sight of him as if he'd evaporated into nothing. He didn't want to ask him about it; that would be creepy. *So, I was following you home last night...* That sentence had no good ending. But nevertheless, his interest was piqued more than ever.

Then midway through July, Mac didn't show up to work for a week. Everything else was in its place. The bats covered in chocolate-colored pine tar. The gloves and uniforms held a certain layer of dirt, like they'd all soaked in carrot juice overnight. Piney, the mascot, was in his absurd, billowing-tree costume with the googly eyes that never stopped moving.

The signs bolted to the outfield wall advertised businesses like Jeremiah's Fish Fry, Merkin's Wig Emporium, and The Bird House, home of the famous beer-battered chicken sandwich.

The players on the field scratched every part of their bodies their hands could reach as if the uniforms were burlap, and the manager crouched in the dugout, adding to his lagoon of chaw-stained spit. Everything was in place except the boisterous, pot-bellied man the fans were in attendance for.

They embarked upon Pimlington Grounds, eager and fervent for the game, yet all left the stadium with a sense of discontented frustration. The Evereadys managed hits, and sometimes even wins; some teams were simply too bad to lose to. But nonetheless, they knew something was out of place.

The torrential deluge came early in a game against the Elba City Alabasters, sending the Evergreen enthusiasts awkwardly tearing up the stairs for cover. The scoreless game would be rescheduled for drier weather, having barely made it to the third inning. But the rains never seemed to let up. Or more correctly, they let up, simply to start again right as the team was about to take the field. As if the gods themselves stopped the proceedings.

"*No poet, no play,*" they seemed to say.

One day after the game was called, Jimmy sat with Sol at a booth in the Stealing Home Saloon. The little lamp attached to the wall lit just enough of the table for their secret conversation.

"I'm telling you, Suds. I don't know where he is. One minute, he's throwing back an Olde Timer Ale with us at the bar, then the next, he's *poof*. Gone to who knows where." The large pores on Sol's swollen red nose contrasted his gray-glass eyes—the color faded from them as if his life had come and gone.

"Nobody simply disappears. You don't think he's hurt or anything?"

"If he was, I'm sure his wife would have called the park. Let us know what was going on."

Jimmy sat up straight. "He's got a wife? Neither of you mentioned this before."

Sol stared down at the floor, thumbing his chin. "Gee, ya know. I kinda always assumed he had a wife. Now, I'm not really sure. Hey, Tom, you know if Mac's got a wife?"

Tom sat up at the bar. "Hell, if I know. If he does, I never heard him talk about her."

"Sorry, kid. He just up and left, I guess."

"You've been drinking and working with him for forty years. Suddenly, he's up and gone without so much as a 'smell ya later,' and you're not concerned?" Slightly offended, Jimmy sipped on his bottle of Kromer's Lite.

"Christ. Of course, I'm concerned. Hurt, too. You think you know somebody, and when their gone, you come to realize all you ever talked about with the guy was baseball and beer." The old man stared at the little glowing lamp as his face sank in on itself, aging right before Jimmy's eyes, so he dropped it.

"You think these rains'll ever let up? It's been raining for a week now." The weather was always a safe topic to change gears.

"I hope so. If they don't play, I don't work, and I can't pay the bills. 'Sides, this team needs another rainout like I need a third hernia."

Jimmy grinned, vaguely understanding the man's point. He took another sip of his beer, emptying the bottle. "I'm out. You want another one?"

"Nah. Thanks, but all this talk of wives gots me thinking. I should probably be heading home. Lavern's making lasagna tonight."

"That the lasagna that gave all those orphans the runs?"

"That's the one. Have another one on me. Tom, another beer for the underage brat." He stood up and put down money on the bar. He winked and smiled at Jimmy. Then, he was gone.

Jimmy sat supping his lager in the dim light, studying the various shadowed photographs and newspaper clippings encased in their glass tombs. Above his booth hung the photo of the 1963 Championship team. Row upon row of ballplayers packed in tight on the grandstands at Pimlington Grounds. Their uniforms unsullied, and their smooth faces. Some smiling, some not. Jimmy finished his beer, stood to walk out, and looked at the photo once more.

A set of eyes stared back at him, and Jimmy jumped on the seat to get a closer look.

"Suds, what the *hell*? Why do you think those seats got patched up with tape in the first place?" Tom slapped his damp rag on the bar.

His shoes kicked up the seat's peeling duct tape. "Sorry, Tom. I gotta see something."

He scrutinized every player in the dusty picture. "Christ. I knew it."

There he was, third row back, sixth man in. His gut wasn't shaped yet, and he was missing the mustache, but there he stood, plain as day. The bottom of the photo correlated names to players.

Bob MacGinty.

"Son of a bitch."

The town of Evergreen was like something out of an American fantasy. Many said Norman Rockwell himself visited on occasion for inspiration. Surrounded on all sides by Green Valley's expansive Arbor Sanctuary, Main Street stretched across town as the sole way in or out. From Main Street, the town lingering outward with various side streets lined with quaint homes and block shaped, brick apartment buildings. It was a charming oasis: an absolute contrast to Lakeview, the city to the north.

Evergreen started at one end with the Taste-E-Freeze and the Drive-in movie. Further up Main Street was the Baptist church and the Methodist church. The two structures, both wooden and white, carried competing spires, which appeared to reach record heights each year. The Catholic Church, stone and glass and the tallest structure in town, was at the other end of Main, leading back into the compacted forest. In between the two portals was a town vibrating out with Main Street as its spine.

The businesses were always changing. For a little while, an artisanal cheese shop did well. Some stores came and left before people caught a chance to poke their heads in: Karate dojos, ladies undergarments, custom jewelry, a bike shop, a toy store, and at least one new restaurant every year.

These genuinely kitschy stores lead themselves to the edge of the high school's front lawn. The great building seemed more like a personal residence than a school, surrounded by a thick layer of lush and fresh emerald grass on a high valley hill.

The most consistent stores in town were in the square. The bakery where patrons could always get a decent pie. The Bootery, supplying all of the town's people with the latest fashions. And the Lamp Shade Bar and Grill, where everyone went to watch games on Sunday and teach their sons about football.

Further down the street was Pimlington Grounds, the newspaper office, Town Hall, and The Herman J. Putnam Memorial Library, which was set back with a large promenade of stores around the edges and a tiny grass park with a massive fountain at its center. Red brick paths crisscrossed the grassy lawn. In front, a stone courtyard surrounded another smaller fountain.

From the bottom of the stairs, the library appeared like an imposing religious temple. Each of the chiseled granite stairs providing a different literary quote, slippery from the uninvited rain, soaking everything and everyone to their breaking points. Greek columns held up a formidable isosceles roof.

Jimmy rarely saw people go into the library, which was odd, being that it was easily the most impressive building in town. With the rain coming down hard again, he hurried inside.

Past the heavy glass doors, he entered another world, as if time stood still. The shades drawn, green and gold table lamps throughout the cavernous halls lit the dim building.

Jimmy walked down the foreboding stairs running under the first floor to the maze known as the Archives Section. On the first landing stood a sign holder with no sign in it. No matter how hard Jimmy tried, each step he took shot a clapping echo that bounced around the underground space. At the foot of the stairs, a room revealed crowded bookshelves overrun by piles of loose paper. Some lights flickered as the venting for the HVAC rumbled, causing a vibration. The aisles ran the length of the room, though Jimmy couldn't make out where they ended. The resulting labyrinth would be easy to get lost in.

Jimmy tripped over a shorter stack of pages at his feet.

The pervading mildew and dusty decay lingered on every page. How dry it felt. Lighting a match would devastate the whole space in seconds. As he navigated his way through the mess, Jimmy finally happened upon the right section.

The intimidating mound was high enough to give Jimmy the sense he'd never find what he came for. Yet, despite his uncertainty, it wasn't long before he discovered that Bob MacGinty was quite the premiere player. In 1964, he helped lead the team to their championship season, boasting a .374 batting average with twenty-two home runs and eighty-six RBI's. Though the means of acquiring information were antiquated, he kept at it, fueled by his passion to know who the mystery ball player really was.

When Jimmy approached Sol with his initial findings, the old man was apathetic at best. Sol'd never knew much about his friend and didn't care to prod into his personal affairs. His actual words were, "None o' my bidness." Notwithstanding Sol's weariness, he recognized the name of MacGinty. The look was enough to feed Jimmy's resolve to find the truth.

As soon as the day's game was canceled, Jimmy hurried back to the archives section of the library. He continued like that for a week, searching, reading, and studying the old faded pictures and articles. He searched through stacks of old musty newspapers, damp and decaying books, and dirty speckled microfiche.

Sol grew irritable and didn't ever want to talk about anything more than baseball and who was buying the next round, tired and drained of life's rigors. Whenever Jimmy brought up Mac, Sol grew upset and walked away.

Jimmy learned that Bob MacGinty was beaned in the head at the beginning of the '65 season. At a time before protective helmets, he lay in a comma for weeks. Though his motor functions were all in tip-top shape, the team wouldn't take the risk of sending him back on the field. Heartbroken, he disappeared.

Coincidentally, after five years of dismal showings, the man that later became known as "The Poet" made his first appearance in Pimlington Grounds in the middle of the 1970 season. The team pulled themselves out of a doomed season to become the wildcard on one of the hottest streaks in recent memory. From that day forward, the Evereadys were unstoppable, making it to the post season fifteen years in a row. No one ever gave a definitive answer as to how they came by their success, perennially posting teams filled with has-beens and never-weres.

Yet in the years to come, the team lost its gusto, appearing in the playoffs once since their years as the hottest team in the Arbor League. The attention shifted from the field to the antics in the stands. No one really cared if the team won or lost as long as they got a chance to see the famed Ballpark Poet.

Although confident he'd discovered the who and what surrounding the mystery of Mac's identity, Jimmy needed to know the why.

"Wieners. Get your foot-long wieners here. Steaming hot brats. Scolding Red Hots here." The hot dog vender's calls reverberated over the crowd. A group of little boys snickered hysterically each time he made another call for wieners.

A drizzle hung over the field. But, until there was thunder and lightning, they weren't going to call the game. The clouds permitted minimal light. A thick blanket of fog slept over the outfield. The night game lights were fired up, despite it only being two in the afternoon. Everything seemed that much more grim.

Jimmy strapped on his ice tub during the first inning, although he figured he wouldn't be wearing it for long, considering the forecast called for heavier rains. As he entered the ballpark, the misery in the faces of the crowd gave him a shiver. Piney was doing a stupid dance on top of the dugout, which kept the attention of a few kids, but left the rest utterly unimpressed. He slipped on the slick surface, crashing down with a hard thud. The children laughed at the clowning mascot as he picked himself up slow, rubbing his funny bone.

A ray of sun shot through and hit Jimmy in the eyes for a second before the clouds swallowed it again.

The Evereadys were down two runs. Jimmy clapped his hands and cheered for the "Emerald Menace." Awkwardly, it echoed throughout the entire stadium. Starting off the bottom of the first, "Mucky" Joe Turner got beaned by a pitch and limped to first base. Turner twisted away as it caught him square in the back, and his face tightened in a wince.

As soon as the ball struck Mucky, Jimmy ceased his cheering. A group of fans glared at him as if he'd caused of the injury.

Jimmy clapped his hands again, this time without the cheers.

Dan "The Tomahawk" Lightfoot cracked a dribbling grounder to first, where he was promptly tagged out. But he did, however, advance the runner.

One out.

From the dugout climbed the largest, most handsome ballplayer the team had ever known. Casey "The Bat" Thayer let the strikes mosey past him as if unaware what he was there to do. He regarded the bat in his hands like some foreign object, and the fans booed with disgust.

The tension finally exploded into what Jimmy later called a last-ditch effort.

"Hey, you there, without a clue. What's round and white and can be thrown in a screw? Instead of one try, you'll get a few. Better take notice, or you'll be yesterday's news." Jimmy paused as a few nearby fans shifted their attention. "Everyone here is sure you know what to do. So while I stand here and sell these people brew, do us a favor and smash one for two."

Casey glared at Jimmy before he smirked and raised the bat proper.

The crowd pelted him with their thoughts.

That's not Mac. What's he think he's doing?

When the next pitch came in, the bat swung, screaming a crack across the stands. The ball sailed through the murk and mist, screaming past the fence, through the clouds, and entered orbit. The skin of the baseball was found in short center—the stitches busted like a madman's torn straightjacket. "The Bat" rounded the bases as the fans shattered their silence in a cheer that shook the stadium. When he crossed home plate, he nodded up at Jimmy and tipped his hat.

The game was tied two all.

Jimmy flushed. His thin frame shook from nerves as he struggled to piece together what happened.

Christ, was that me?

The next batter stepped up to the plate. Boney "Crawdad" Jibsome was as hopeless a player as the Eveready's ever came by. Gangly in all the wrong places, he wore glasses that magnified his eyes. The pitcher, "Catfish" Merchant, sized him up and challenged him with a fastball. The sizzle of the ball cut through the drizzle before the subsequent *snap* of the ball in the catcher's mitt.

Strike one.

The mass of fans waited to see what Jimmy would do, still at the mouth of the entrance. Catfish set himself, pulled the ball back behind his head, and catapulted another snapping fling.

Strike two.

Everyone in the stands shifted their gazes from the plate back to him.

He worked to stir up something else.

"My dear, Crawdad, don't be such a cad. If you keep on your path, you'll be a passing fad. One and one equal two. Can't you add?" The attention narrowed in on Jimmy. "Show these people what they came to see. If you swing the bat, don't make it three. Don't tell us we need to pinch the tail and suck the head to see you hit and break the threads." The crowd let out some chuckles, and Jimmy swelled.

Crawdad swatted his hand at Jimmy, as if to say shut up. But he might have just as easily been swatting at a gnat buzzing in his ear.

Catfish wound up and released a cannonball.

Crawdad swung with a clumsy swipe and hit the ball high. It arched and broke slightly foul. Still alive.

A little boy sitting in a row next to Jimmy looked up with his wide hopeful eyes. "Do it again."

Jimmy nodded at the boy. "Crawdad, Crawdad, you can do better than that. Extend your back arm and follow through with the bat." Jimmy was as interested as everyone else to see what might happen.

Hell, if Mac can do it, why not me?

The next pitch came in with a familiar clap.

Later, people would say, "Crawdad put everything he had into that swing," and they were right. The bat and ball connected with a loud *crack*, pulsing throughout the park. The ball flew over the first baseman and into a particularly difficult corner of right field the fans christened as Tiny's Knot.

The right fielder sprinted for the ball but slipped on the slick grass and came crashing into the barrier.

Crawdad hesitated for a second, having been so long since he last made contact, and set off rounding first.

The right fielder was down, holding his arm as he rolled in the umber mud.

The center fielder galloped over as backup.

Crawdad passed second in long accentuated awkward strides.

The center fielder picked up the ball and hurled it home, but it slipped out of his hand and only reached the second baseman.

The keystone bagger griped the ball and threw as Crawdad broke for home, converging with the catcher the instant the ball touched leather. In the collision of the two men, limbs flailed as Crawdad bowled over home plate, and the wet ball slipped loose.

The mob detonated, waking up old-man Winkle, living across the street.

Surpassing the visitors, the Evereadys led three to two.

The ensuing mania sent everyone to their feet, hugging complete strangers, and brought a few grown men to tears.

"You did it." The little boy cheered.

Chest tight, Jimmy struggled to take in a full breath. He tore back down the gangway for air.

What was that? No way that happened.

But the cheers from the crowd told a different story.

"How is any of that even possible?"

"You channeled the gods, Suds. How'd ya think it happened?"

Jimmy jumped to find an empty corridor.

"Who said—"

"I did, kid." Mac towered over him in the void. "You did damn well for your first attempt, too."

"Mac, where the hell have you—"

"Around. Listen, kid. This is gonna be hard for you to understand. Hell, I've been doing it for over forty years, and I have a hard time with it myself." He'd aged, faded like a worn picture. The lines on his face deepened, and the light in his eyes had all but gone out.

"Mac, I know who you are."

"About time. Any longer, and we might not have had a shot at the wild card. I'm all spent, Suds. Used up. The rhymes are still there, but the magic's gone. Once, I willed balls out of the park with a few verses, no sweat off my back. Now, I can't even manage a winning record." He looked away in shame. "It's your turn. Team needs you."

"I don't understand. What do you mean, 'My first time? The team needs me?'"

"You found me out. You discovered my secret. Team's yours now."

"You're not talking sense here. Baseball doesn't work that way. *Reality* doesn't work that way."

"What you think baseball is and isn't doesn't matter. Baseball, for lack of a better word, is a religion. It's got gods and heroes and epic battles that end in historic miracles. People go to the park for the spectacle, just like they go to church. You can listen to a preacher on the radio or read the Bible at home. But you go to church to be with God. Same's true with baseball."

"But it's just a game."

"Ask Ralph Branca or poor Fred Merkle. Ask Bill Buckner—or even Steve-fricking-Bartman if it's just a game. Any sport that has the power to ruin a man is far more than *just* a game. I assure you, there *are* baseball gods. They rained on Wrigley their first attempt at a night game. They made it possible for Ruth's called shot. They were there with DiMaggio throughout his hitting streak. And Maris for his, too. Certainly gave Robinson the strength to make it through his first couple years. They give, and they take. They'll make a premiere slugger go oh-for-twenty, and they can make a nobody—like Crawdad—hit an inside-the-park home run." He feigned swinging a bat, his lead hand then gesturing to the field. "They simply need their conduit. You, my friend, are it. For the Evereadys, anyhow."

He tapped the brim of Jimmy's hat.

"So you're telling me that whether the 'Readys win or lose rests on my shoulders?" Jimmy's head spun.

"In a matter of speaking, yeah. Really, it's the crowd. You simply get them to where they need to be. Just like me. Recognized it in you the instant I saw you. You influence and channel their enthusiasm. They do the rest. I know how crazy it sounds, but you'll get the hang of it. Keep their attention on the field, and you'll be fine." He patted Jimmy on the shoulder.

"So, what, you're leaving now? What about Sol? Aren't you gonna say goodbye?"

"Sol? Who d'you think passed it to me? I'm not going anywhere, kid. Just stepping down as The Poet." Mac swung his doorknob nose toward the field as he heard a loud *snap*. "Watch yer head."

A foul ball careened into the corridor. Jimmy ducked out of the way, spilling some of the water from his beer tub. When he righted himself, Mac was gone.

Jimmy picked up the ball and walked back up the ramp into the park. The sun shone bright now, hardly a cloud in the sky. The batter was fighting off Catfish with a full count. Jimmy gave the foul ball to the little boy who'd had so much faith in him earlier.

"Thanks, mister." The boy's face beamed at his new gift.

The crowd hushed when they saw Jimmy reemerge. Every face in the park stared at him. As he scanned the fans, he found Mac and Sol standing in the mouth of a gangway on the other side of the stadium. Both gave him a wink and a smile.

And like that, his words spilled out across the park.

"Full count, full count. A rally's on the mount." He honed in on the pitcher atop his mound. "Hey, Catfish, you should call it a day. If you stay in, you'll lead your team astray."

Smiles materialized on the fans.

"Don't give up the lead. The 'Readys'll make ya bleed."

The resulting cheer was all he needed to know he was on to something.

Catfish sneered and spit in Jimmy's direction. The new Poet was already under the pitcher's skin. Catfish wound up and vaulted the ball toward the plate.

Crack. The clouds parted and the ball sailed into legend.

IV.

In the tiny town of Evergreen, a tradition exists: a rite of passage amongst the young men in town. They prove their manhood by gathering at the Main St. entrances of the Arbor Sanctuary. Due to the thick foliage surrounding the strip of road, drivers can hardly see a few yards in front of them until fully emerged from the dense wood. Knowing this, the boys strip down to their shorts, crouch low, kissing the pavement, and at the last possible moment, they leap like frogs in front of oncoming traffic to the opposite side of the street.

Over the years, many a boy has been lost to this ritual, jumping too late or too slow or simply not high enough. And, over the years, parents and councilmen, teachers and loved ones have all campaigned against the feat of idiocy.

Nonetheless, each summer, the boys sneak from their homes late at night, challenging one another to make the Leap of Faith. If successful, a boy can transform himself, attaining status as a living legend for the rest of his days. For those who aren't, their blood stains the mouth of the portal as a legacy to their adolescent bravery and childish folly.

On such a night, a boy, who was picked on in school for being too thin and gangly, decided to change the tide of his life. And he might have been successful had he gone any other night. For none other than Jinx Jenkins rested on the bench of the Taste-E-Freeze, watching the boy prepare to jump.

Jinx knew what the boy was about to do, so he called to wish him some luck.

The boy jumped, the mark of Jinx sticking to him in mid-flight.

He rolled over the top of a worn-down, old station wagon.

Jinx vanished by the time the boy found his way back to the pavement.

MADDEST MIDSUMMER'S NIGHT

WILL S. (05:03 PM)
Anyone know how these new bags work?

DISPATCH (05:04 PM)
You need to make sure you plug it into your car adapter, or the thing will die on you, and you won't be able to receive orders.

WILL S. (05:04PM)
Right, I did that, but what about this display? Is there any way to set it to English, or do I just need to learn Japanese?

DISPATCH (05:06 PM)
Will, it should always be set to English. I'm not sure what your problem is.

WILL S. (05:06 PM)
My problem is that the way things are *supposed* to be and the way things are *actually* working aren't matching up. My display is supposed to be in English. My

display is actually in Japanese. How do I change this?

ROB G. (05:08 PM)
Hey, Willy boy. Puck, here. Listen. Same thing happened to me this morning when I took it out of the packaging. Look at the display. You see the button that says MENU? Push it until you see the icon of a flag. When you find that, arrow down to English, and press the big round OK button in between the arrows.

WILL S. (05:12 PM)
Got it. Thanks, Puck. Why doesn't technology ever work the way it's supposed to?

ROB G. (05:12 PM)
You know I got your back.

DISPATCH (05:15 PM)
Puck, just a reminder, your shadow should be arriving soon. Let us know when he gets there, and we'll shoot you an order.

ROB G. (05:15 PM)
Ten Four.

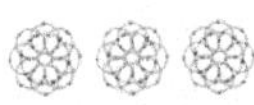

What's the craziest night I ever had on the job, you ask? Let me tell you about my first night as a delivery driver for ChowNow.

Puck sat parked next to a fire hydrant with his hazard lights flashing. I approached his sad, old station wagon, waiting for me in the halo of a stark streetlight. He was listening to the Eveready's and Lumber Jacks in the fifth inning with his window cracked. Under it laid a scattered pile of sunflower seed shells. The car hissed—creaking, ticking, and gurgling. Despite the streetlamp above, the dark hid the color of the car. Mud Pink, Regrettable Red, Oxidized Orange, maybe Barely-a-Color Blue?

He picked me up in front of Four Shadows Bar and Grill. I really didn't know what to make of him at first. He wore his '08 Timber Ridge High School varsity jacket and a Pork Pie hat.

I tapped on the window.

"You the novice?" he asked, rolling it down.

"Marty. Yeah, you're Robin?"

"Rob. They call me Puck." Young but seasoned, his face reminded me of a postcard I once found at a truck stop of a baby with a five o'clock shadow. A slight belly protruded from his jacket, and a scar crossed his upper lip.

"Let me get this out of your way so you can sit down." He plopped in the passenger seat and came out holding a giant red fabric bag with black handles, placing it gently in the back seat thick with a bed of garbage, and making sure to keep it level. Paper bags, empty plastic bottles, and wrappers fell out onto the street. He gathered them up and threw them back in the car.

"This'll be interesting tonight. We just got these new delivery bags shipped out to us. Pretty cool. Cuts out the middle man." He was a handsome kid when he wasn't talking. Unfortunately, he never shut up.

He smirked. "Planning on selling Bibles tonight?"

The window's reflection showed me next to Puck, out of place with my button up shirt and tie, hair parted on the side, and my lack of stubble. I told my girlfriend delivery drivers don't wear ties, but she insisted I make a good impression on the first day. Figures.

"First impressions…never mind." I really didn't want to get into it with him.

"Whatever."

I sat, and he drove. The front dash was much different than the exterior. A pair of fuzzy die hung from the rearview mirror with a Lakeview Leviathans logo on them. A series of tablets and smart phones were mounted at all different angles. He touched one and played classic 80's pop. Another one read out sports scores, and his phone opened to an app, showing no outstanding orders.

"As I was saying, we don't have to waste our time anymore going to a restaurant. Food comes straight to the bag, and we go to the address on the display. The bag and my phone are synched." I glanced at the bag again; a large rectangle in the center of the lid was full of buttons and had a bright digital display. "The way it works is a person orders food by phone or online. The order is sent to the restaurant, the restaurant makes the food, then we get the food sent to the bag."

I waited for him to explain the final process, but he just drove recklessly, swerving around slow cars, rolling past stop signs, squeezing into traffic when there wasn't enough space.

"So, how exactly does the food get in the bag?" I finally asked.

"I just told you, the restaurant sends it to us, then we take it to the customer." A car in front of him came to a stop.

"*Cock sucking cum bucket.*"

Instead of slowing down, he squeezed around the car, shooting through the stoplight. My fingers lashed out to take hold of a handle but couldn't find one.

"The first rule to this job is speed. The quicker you get the order to the customer, the more orders you'll get. Equals the more money you make." I could tell he was trying to impress me.

But his confident recklessness had an adverse effect.

"Right, but how do they send it?"

"How the fuck should I know? You gotta phone?" I pulled out my latest model from BigCorp. "Great. So you get calls on the fucker, right?"

"Yeah."

"But do you know how you receive calls on it?"

"Actually—"

"My point exactly. Everyone's got a phone these days. Does anybody actually know how it works? Nope. Just works, until it doesn't." He sounded assured in his line of reasoning. Much the way I imagined Socrates when he came up with all that sands of time stuff.

"So, it's like magic?"

He stared at me blankly, not looking at traffic, yet still avoided two bikers and person in a wheelchair. As if he knew every move happening around him. "I'm sorry?"

"Yeah, Arthur C. Clarke said that any sufficiently advanced technology is indistinguishable from magic."

His face pursed in laughter. "Great, I'm training Mr.-fuckin-Wizard here. Yeah. I guess if that's the way you want to look at it, it's like magic."

Bing. The bag chimed, and the red light blinked.

"Do me a favor and reach back there and tell me what the display says? Usually, I keep it where you're sitting, so I don't have to look so far." As I twisted around in my seat, he swerved around a biker, and I rolled into him a bit. "Watch it, Novice. Driving is a delicate art in this city."

I read him the address as he typed it out on his phone's GPS, and the time for delivery—fifteen minutes—as he narrowly veered out of the way of some pedestrians who started drifting into the street. "Fuckin Walkers."

"Excuse me?" I struggled back into my seat.

"Pedestrians back there, came out of nowhere. One thing I realized when I started this job, everyone's got a group. You might have a couple. You might not even realize you've got one at all. But sure as shit, you've got one. Especially when it comes to driving. And what's worse is, they don't realize it, but they are *all* out to fuck with you and make you late." The slightest bit of paranoia laced his voice. I had an uncle like that. He got electroshock every weekend to even him out.

"Walkers wander into the street and assume everyone knows they're there. Doesn't matter if there's a crosswalk or not. They just go." We sped down narrower streets, lined with row houses and apartment buildings. He hit a speed hump at full force, and I knocked my head on the roof. At the next intersection, he turned right with no blinker.

"Then, you've got bikers, or Psychos. Fuckers are forced to ride on the street, but they don't pay any attention to the rules of the road. Stop sign, they blow through if it's their turn or not. They never let you know when they're about to turn, and they're always taking up my entire goddamn lane. Swear to God, they all have a fucking death wish." Puck leaned over and reached into his center console, pulling out a baggie of gummy bears. He offered me some.

"No, thanks." Who knew what microscopic atrocities lingered under his dirty finger nails.

"Suit yourself. Second rule to this job is always have snacks. You're gonna be in the car up to ten hours. They might give you a break, but sometimes, they don't. My favorites are gummy bears and sunflower seeds. You know, something small to graze on. Usually, I go in and get a couple bags, then dump them all into one big bag, so I don't have to refill as much. Basically, from now on, energy drinks and sugar are your best friends."

I kicked at an assortment of candy wrappers, receipts, and tall metal cans. *When was the last time he cleaned out his car?*

"As far as other drivers go, you've got buses who are simply doing their best. I call 'em Whales. Be nice to 'em. Sure, they get in the way. And God help you if you get stuck behind one. But for the most part, they're trying to get from one stop to the next without being cut off by every motherfucker in existence. My dad was a bus driver, so I've got a soft spot for 'em." His façade dropped as he reflected on it but promptly resumed.

"Go suck a tailpipe, you queef gone wrong." Puck threw a quaking bird at a car not letting him merge.

We came to a stoplight, and he pointed at a person going the other direction. "You've also got Out-of-Towners, who are always lost, and for some reason, always from Ohio."

The light changed, and we passed the car. The plates said Ohio.

"Then, there's the soccer moms who are all driving tanks you should have a special license to operate. Self-righteous bitches, the lot of 'em. Practically every time I've been cut off while in the 'burbs, it's been by a soccer mom. But you've also got truckers, maintenance vans, and police. Any one of them will cut you off and not realize it. Or give a shit."

As if on cue, he pulled over, and an ambulance rushed past us.

"Here's a tip," he said as he swung back into traffic. "Any time you pull over for emergency vehicles, and they're going the same way as you, make sure to pull back into traffic the second they pass. If you wait too long, you might get caught there. And if you do it just right, you might be able to use the ambulance as your personal escort. But don't follow too close. They hate that."

"I believe it's actually illegal—"

"Biggest fuck-heads are the cabbies. Either they're going way too fast, or entirely too slow. Never in between. They'll pull a U-turn in front of you without any warning, troll for potential passengers in heavy traffic, or come to a complete stop in the middle of the fucking road. I can't even tell you how many deliveries I've had go late because some shit stain in a hybrid decided to haggle over his fare with his customer. And they're rude fuckers, too. They're always honking at you a split-second after the light changes. They always look pissed, like they're eternally smelling dog shit. And what's worse is they've got these independent drivers, too, with Ryde and whatnot. They're even crappier drivers because they don't have anybody to report back to. God, I fucking hate cabbies."

"Aren't we considered independent contractors?" I was no fan of taxi drivers myself. But his reasoning grew harder for me to make sense of.

"Yeah, but at least we give you newbies a few hours of training. These guys'll rear end you and not even stop to see the damage. *Oh, look at me in my big black SUV. I'm so special, and everyone should trust me.* Nothing sketchy at all about getting into a complete stranger's car."

"My sister has a theory all people that drive black SUV's are assholes." Probably best to agree with him.

"After driving delivery for a few years now, I can wholeheartedly tell you she's got a point. Black SUV's and white pickup trucks." He considered me for the first time as though we were finally on the same wavelength. "Everyone's got something to prove. No one knows who they're proving it to."

Finally, we veered down a one-way residential street, and he slowed the car to a crawl. I let go of the arm rests, my fingerprints had left indents in the colored vinyl. He took a look at the address again and rolled down the street. "One of the problems you get at night is that you can't see shit. Half the places you're attempting to find don't have their lights on, and the other half don't even have numbers on the building."

The street brimmed with cars, leaving us nowhere to park. Puck sidled up to the fire hydrant again and threw on his hazards. "Rule three: when you see a fire hydrant, consider it your own personal delivery parking spot. And if the street is wide enough, don't be afraid to double park. It's kind of industry standard."

More trash spilled out as he opened the back, and he scooped it back inside. As he lifted the bag's lid, I half expected fairy dust and twinkling stars. *What could this bag be? What was it made of? Was the inside a grid of wires and electrical current? Broadcasting molecules? Would it change the food at all?*

All I saw was padded black plastic siding.

A let down.

Inside was a half-filled brown paper bag with a handle.

How the fuck did the food get in there?

He closed the lid, which beeped again, and the red light lit up.

"We're in business tonight. So, Novice, when we get to the residence, we simply make sure we grab the right order, go to the buzzer, find the name, and wait to be let in. Or sometimes, they come down and get the food themselves." He spoke like he was explaining how to split atoms.

We walked up to the door's metal box. "What'd you say the name was on this?"

"Erica Jensing, 13B." He found the name, she buzzed us in, and we pushed our way past the two glass double doors in the front entrance. Covered in peeling wood laminate, the elevator's ceiling lacked paneling and the exposed florescent light growled a low hum. His face clearer, the lighting offered him zero favors. His face full of whiskers and acne and dried scabs.

The floors dinged past as we gained altitude. Finally, it stopped, and we stepped into a dimmed hall. Better lighting for the both of us, but we were blasted with the funk of curry and body odor.

Puck manically searched the numbers on the doors. "They never organize these buildings with any rhyme or reason. Some start with the first apartment then whip around. Some are evens on one side, odds on the other. And then, there's the idiots that start the numbers at the far end of the hall and work up to the elevator. Swear to God, not a single building I've ever been in is the same, which leaves you looking like a tard as you try and find your way around the floor."

We found 13B and Erica Jensing.

"Erica?" Puck elbowed me. "You always want to verify the person you're handing the food to."

"Yeah." She was a short blond in a sweatshirt with large colorful Greek letters on it. Beta Kappa Eta. BCH to you and I. She was pretty, but in the way you only recognize after she's done herself up. Her face was 90% scowl, 10% whatever's left. "You're late. My email said you'd be here by 6:42. It's 6:44."

She glanced down at her watch to prove it.

My watch read only 6:38.

"We are very sorry about that, ma'am. Had to wait for some kids to cross the street at the children's hospital." She rolled her eyes as Puck handed her the food and paused, pressing her with his willful gaze.

"Is that it?" she said as if we ruined her day.

"Actually, ma'am, it says here that you had specified a cash tip online." Puck held his phone to show her where it said "TIP—Cash."

She shrugged and backed away. "I did no such thing."

He showed it to her again. "I'm sorry, ma'am, but you did. You can't accidentally specify a cash tip on the website. You have to make a conscious decision to click on the cash tip option."

"I don't care. You're a liar. Whatever."

"Wow. You're a bit—" She slammed the door in Puck's face. He flushed, angry. "Can you believe this *bitch*? Fucking *cunt*. I swear, every time I get stiffed, it's by some entitled *white rich bitch*. Probably hasn't ever had to work for a living in her life. Sure, she has a job, but her daddy pays *all the fucking bills*."

He yelled at the door more than me, reaching in his jacket and pulling out a permanent marker to write.

I GIVE FREE BJ's. JUST KNOCK.

He called back to her as we left. "Erica Jensing in 13B is a no-tipping whore. Erica Jensing doesn't tip. Erica Jensing of 13B gives free BJ's."

When we returned to the car, he typed rapidly on his phone.

I didn't know if I should laugh or hide from the police.

Puck was touched in the most entertaining way possible. I wanted to write tonight off as a loss, but something said to stay. The wave of excitement, the rush of fear. I was hooked.

He had me.

What the hell was he writing?

It was the longest he'd shut up all night.

This guy really had some balls. I respected him because of it.

After he was done typing, he mounted his phone on the dash again. "There. She'll think again before stiffing a delivery guy."

"What'd you do?"

"I posted her name and phone number on FaceSpace. Told my friends to text and call her about being a complete twat waffle." He beamed at his handiwork, tipping his hat back on his head.

"Wow, you're kind of *off*, you know that?" Half of me was appalled, and the other half was jealous I hadn't thought of it.

This guy might be my new hero.

"Yeah, I know. Ain't it great." He threw the car into drive and sped toward the next delivery.

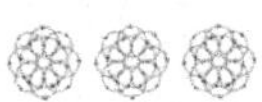

He flew through the night with grace and finesse, adapting to each situation on the street like a dogfighting pilot. When the two-way road narrowed with parked cars, he barreled headlong into the infinitesimal pocket of road that separated himself from the oncoming traffic.

He never blinked.

Doubt if his heart sped up. Or maybe it always beat fast with the energy drinks and sugar.

Most of the orders I shadowed were pretty quick. In, hand off the food, out.

The orders picked up. Around 7:30, the bag chimed every couple of minutes. Each time we opened the lid, more and more paper and plastic bags were waiting to be delivered.

Puck took alleys as shortcuts. Said they were like his own private roadways the rest of the city hadn't caught on to. As we sped past the garages and trashcans, the music blared.

Down one, a woman on the second story porch talked down to a giant with an axe. The guy was huge. Larger than anyone I'd ever seen.

When I turned to take a second look, he was gone.

The constant speed must have gotten to me. I was hallucinating.

It was Lakeview though.

Weird shit went down on every block.

All you had to do was choose to notice.

Every time an order specified a cash tip, he waited just long enough, and the customer was sure to hand off the money. Once, the guy pulled the same deal as Erica and pretended not to remember he'd specified the cash tip option. Puck started into the same spiel as before, only this time it worked.

I finally asked him about it in the car.

"So, you actually ask for the tip? You don't think that's a little too…brazen?"

A stoplight slowed him to a halt. "Novice, Marty, let me explain something to you. They can't accidentally specify a cash tip. A lot of them click on it and figure I'll be a pushover, and they won't need to pay me. Little do they know… The way I figure it, we've both gone into this with a simple social contract. I bring their lazy, agoraphobic ass dinner, and they give me a couple of bucks for the trouble. If I fulfill my end, they sure as shit better do theirs."

"Right, but you realize that tipping is a courtesy. Not mandatory." I understood his point, but his logic always seemed skewed.

"Novice. You drive around Green Valley every day for a few weeks on ten-hour shifts with these gas prices and tell me that tipping is optional. Once you get stiffed, you'll see. We're like any waiter in a restaurant but to an extreme level. Not only do you get to enjoy the comfort of your home and not have to deal with a crowded restaurant, but we get you the food on our own dime. We pay for our own gas. If they tip anything less than two bucks, we lose money on the transaction. The least a customer can do is tip. Sure, it's not mandatory. I know that. But, when we're getting paid $2.75 an order, we need to be assertive about how we get our money. I'm not going to have my power shut off because Mr. and Mrs. Cheapskate decide they waited a few minutes longer than they believed they should." He believed every damn word.

Each syllable he espoused made me want to follow in his footsteps.

I didn't know if I had the balls to treat people that way.

The light changed, and we drove again.

Bing. Another order.

"Take a look back there and see where that one's going."

I read the address on the monitor. "Says it's going somewhere in Evergreen. That can't be right."

"Evergreen? No, no, check it again. That's a good thirty minutes out of our way."

"Yep. That's what it says. 1495 Pimlington Way, Evergreen. Twenty-five minutes until delivery."

"*Jesus Christ*." He pulled over and opened the Dispatch app.

ROB G. (08:09 PM)

Hey, dispatch, I just got an order that needs to be delivered in Evergreen. I'm currently in the city, around Bridgeport. Nowhere near Evergreen. Please advise.

DISPATCH (08:11 PM)

Puck, that's not right. We see you on our monitors right here. Says you're in the heart of Evergreen right now.

ROB G. (08:11 PM)

Well, I'm not.

DISPATCH (08:12 PM)
You are, too, Puck. We see you right there on our…oh. Wait. Oops. I, uh. Please standby.

"These assholes are always screwing the pooch, I swear. Not sure where they get them, but none of 'em knows the first thing about the city, driving, or how to breathe without swallowing their own tongues."

DISPATCH (08:13 PM)
Hey, Puck. Yeah, we fucked that up. Got you mixed up with Rob C. The order should have gone to him instead.

ROB G. (08:14 PM)
No problem. Just zap the fucker back or transfer it or whatever.

DISPATCH (08:14 PM)
About that. You're gonna need to deliver the meal. We can only send food once. Otherwise, it gets all "copy of a copy" and doesn't taste right.

ROB G. (08:15 PM)
You're serious with this shit. You guys know that's gonna lay me up for at least a full hour. Getting there and getting back. Learn your fuckin jobs, damn it.

DISPATCH (08:15 PM)
Still within the delivery radius, Puck. Just do it for now. We'll *learn our jobs* later.

We zoomed and zipped through the traffic in the city in the station wagon. The meal had an address in the suburbs, Evergreen, miles down the road. Puck took the Main Street exit out of the city, down the twisty turns of the valley, and through Timber Ridge—a tiny town, as were all settlements in Green Valley County.

From the inclined basin, the road zigzagged its way down.

Below, the clustered lights of the tiny villages resembled constellations in the thick tree cover.

As we grew closer to Evergreen, the woods grew more and more dense until we drove through an arched tunnel of bowed and hunched trees.

We were in the Arbor Sanctuary. Main Street only reached as far as the next turn. All assortment of wildlife sprang from the forest, making me especially cautious.

Puck, however, took each curve with acceleration; every straightaway like a drag race.

I gripped the plastic armrests again. "So, they put the food in the delivery box, type in directions, then the meal is duplicated in our delivery bags? Am I getting this right?"

"I guess. Like I said before, don't ask me the science behind it. I just know it works. As long as they send it to the right driver, that is." He coughed a defeated chuckle. "Why do they do this? Dispatch is always giving restaurants a bigger and bigger radius to up profits. But a larger radius simply means they're gonna have more late deliveries."

He took another sharp turn, one handed this time, and grabbed for his phone.

Five minutes.

The radio reported on the Eveready's and Jack's game, which was well over. Eveready's pulled it off, three-to-two. Puck switched it to a playlist, pumping in through one of his many tablets. I read the names as he swiped through to find the right song. It was classic rock, the whole spectrum from Booker T. & The MG's to Depeche Mode and everything in between. The Rolling Stones' "Time Is On My Side" played, rather fittingly, as Puck's phone counted down.

Four minutes.

He raced about town, employing every shortcut he knew along the way. Samurai-intensity surged across his eyes, like a fat kid in the throes of an ice cream withdrawal.

God knows I wasn't going to be the one to break his concentration.

Puck adjusted his hat, tucking his hair behind his ears. "I'm sure they didn't mention this in your interview, but ChowNow is in the midst of a buyout. Jerry, the guy who started the website, has been talking with BigCorp. Word on the street is we're all gonna end up being full-on employees… just like everybody else. Fucking hypocrite. Jerry was all about the idea of building his business and keeping us independent in the process. I was his first driver, you know. At first, Jerry was on dispatch, and I was in my wagon. We started out small. Took baby steps. We grew it to what it is today. Been by his side the whole damn time. Fucker. Probably gonna take the money and forget I ever existed. Leaving me with what? A BigCorp polo and a pay cut? They'll probably make me paint my car, too."

"*Probably* make you clean up all the trash as well," I said nudging a plastic bottle by my feet. He didn't catch my tone.

"Yeah, wouldn't doubt it. At one point, we were supposed to be full fucking partners. Now, Jerry won't even take my calls."

Drawing closer to Evergreen, the dense woods opened, like a mouth we would be regurgitated from. Puck stepped hard on the gas, and the motor rumbled as we barreled toward the light at the end of the tunnel.

Right as we passed through the aperture of the forest, a young boy ran across the road.

The car slammed into him.

He rolled along the hood, splintering my side of the windshield, and over the roof.

Puck screeched on the brakes.

The boy lay a few feet behind the car. His face was a mess of acne and cuts. A stream of blood ran out his nose. His eyes motionless, staring into the night sky. Dead.

"What do we do?"

For the first time all night, Puck had nothing to say.

V.

There are places in this world that attach themselves to the people who reside in them. When enough life, ample souls, and an abundance of unadulterated emotion find their way into the fabric of a place, it comes alive. It feels the joy and the despair of the folk. In some cases, as much as any member of the community. People come to rely on such a location. They associate it with the greatest chapters of their lives, drawn to the site as if spawning homeward on opening nights.

In Green Valley, one such place was The Grand theater.

Right there, beside the box office, Jinx Jenkins asked his wife, in another life, to marry him. Those were good days. Cleaner, sweeter, happier days when his eyes were sober and his words were clear.

Yes, those were great days; he patted the old ornate columns covered in dust from the renovations already underway.

Later that night, the Old Lady responded to the dejection of her people, sacrificing herself for the safety of their souls.

REEL LIFE

The lights on the marquee shined in a dazzling dance of up and down, off-on-off, twinkling and pulsing—a beacon to humanity. The letters proudly announced "Grand Re-Opening" as the new staff readied the theater for the public. Green Valley's one place of refuge from the putrid fog that filled the air, The Grand situated itself in the exact middle of Main Street in Blisterwood.

Down the street were storefronts, half-filled. Over the years, they changed ownership. Some switched from retail to restaurant and back so many times that every store on Main Street was retrofitted and zoned for just about any business that possessed the courage to brave the fog. Of them, only The Grand stayed put. Not always with the same ownership, either. But it certainly had been there since the beginning of time.

Elmore Pibbs backed out Martin's Donut Shop's door with his rump and walked across the street, double chocolate and coconut in his mouth.

The Grand's conical sign reached above the town like a church steeple. At the top, a globe rotated, illuminated and iridescent, beckoning the attention of the entire valley. On the rare clear night, you could see The Grand all the way from BigCorp Tower in Lakeview.

Elmore's large glasses fogged up with the blue haze as he pirouetted through the sparse morning traffic on its way into the city. His black and gray polyester work shirt itched around his neckline. A smattering of tiny red blotches formed a necklace of pain irritating his freshly shaven stubble.

The sun sprouted over the valley mountains, spilling down into pockets of light and shadow. The streetlamps flickered off as the new day of commerce emerged. Once a one-man toll with beautiful brass spirals and leaves running its edges, the ticket booth stood solitary in a half-domed ivory entryway lined with floral inlays and brilliant yellow bulbs. After the sale, they expanded the booth to house three men, but even that wasn't enough as lines formed down the block.

The ticket stand and the entryway were the first things to go when they sold the The Grand to the MegaPix, a division of BigCorp. Before Elmore got a chance to save them, they were discarded in a heap of broken parts, the guts of the theater strewn about the sidewalk.

Elmore reached into his jacket and fumbled with his large ring of keys. He unlocked the door and slipped inside, past the new eight-man aquarium they'd built as a replacement, fully digitized, modern, and uninspiring.

At first, the lobby was a great cavernous void that could have held anything, even with the bouncing lights of the marquee on all night.

Elmore flipped the line of switches one at a time to reveal the hollowed-out shell of a once sacred place. Two chandeliers previously hung from the ceiling like giant breasts easing patrons in for a warm, tender embrace of a new world or life, but were now replaced by cardboard cutouts advertising the latest releases. Two large, elliptical staircases still ran along the walls. Yet, the walls padded with velvet, silk and gold, as well as the gold-filigree-and-chrome-plated-glass boxes that encased the sweets were long gone. They'd even used an antique popcorn popper the locals said tasted better than the newer ones. The older machine required tending to the kernels with love and attention. Now, everything was streamlined and set to a timer.

Townsfolk dubbed The Grand as the Old Lady because they felt they were in a timeworn, affluent noble woman's home. Which meant always being on their best behavior. Men wore suits, women wore dresses, and children knew better than to scream and cry.

The chain theaters moved in and owners were eventually forced to sell to keep the Old Lady from falling into ruin.

The changes meant the ornate displays of Swingo Candy's latest creations became flashing digital signs with moving background animation. They still sold Swingo, as it, too, was acquired by BigCorp, but they also sold gourmet artisanal sausages, gluten-free ice cream, truffle fries, and the ever-favorite gallon-sized collectors cup of soda with free refills.

Why order a plain, old hot dog and soda when you could order the far more appetizing Number Four? Or perhaps a Number Six, instead of simply ordering candy and popcorn. Everything needed to be bundled, as they constantly tried to sell you things you didn't want, in sizes you didn't need, "For only fifty cents more." Whatever happened to a *reasonable* bag of popcorn, and a *normal*-sized cup?

Their uniforms were once made of a custom-tailored red felt jacket given out to every incoming lobby boy. They wore it with pride along with a red button-on bowtie and the red boxed cap with elastic string.

But as time moved on and people stopped going to the movies as much, the budget for new uniforms dried up, and the theater was left with a handful of jackets, tattered and worn, passed down to each new lobby boy over the next thirty years. This, of course, resulted in some highly comical combinations of tall boys with tiny jackets and small boys drowning within their lapels. Eventually, in the mid '70s, they changed the uniform to a white button up and black pants. But they shared the red button-on bowtie throughout the ages.

These days they wore terrible ill-fitting shirts that Elmore swore were made of burlap. What else in God's name could possibly be so damn itchy?

He coveted the days when they made movies to change things. The movies that dared to scream at a restless American landscape and demand, "Why not?" Elmore longed for the friends he'd once known so intimately. His black and white friends, trapped in celluloid for all time. He spent every waking moment of his childhood watching all the old prints they owned to the point of near ruin.

As an old man, he wondered if these new digital contraptions could capture the real visceral emotion of the actors. The love, the hate, the hurt, and the always-popular betrayal. Would it show through these computers emoting their zeroes and ones? Would they catch the soul the way they did on film?

He didn't trust them.

He made his way up the left side of the double staircase they couldn't figure out how to remove. The sole detail remaining of the Old Lady clinging to the past, her vestigial ribcage. The lights burned in a domino-like succession, illuminating the hallways, the bathrooms, the stairs, and the Exit signs.

Elmore made sure everything was ready for the morning crew. When everything was in its appropriate place, he opened the hidden side door and disappeared into the darkness.

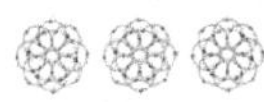

The projection booth had been Elmore's home for forty years. He'd taken the job as a teen in the early '60s when his predecessor and mentor, Todd Harken, retired. From his little perch, he watched as great big-budgeted studio pictures gave way to the French New Wave, as names like Hawks and Wilder were replaced by Peckinpaw and Kubrick. Then, themselves replaced by Scorcese and Spielberg. How the audience jumped in their seats when they first met *Jaws*, and the shock on their faces when they walked out of *The Exorcist*. The way the young girls came back night after night to see Rhett Butler force himself on Scarlett O'Hara. And the twinkle that showed up on everyone's face when Dorothy clicked her magic slippers.

Life had gone on inside those walls, too. Billy Wilkins kissed Rita Lee in the third row during the middle of *Black Beauty*. Tina Shortwinger broke up with Bobby Hertz after he'd attempted the legendary boner through the bottom of the popcorn box trick. The same result transpired for Joe Ramirez, Tony Fastatucci, Brian Cross, and Terrance Wilkes. Mike

Donavan was slapped so many times, his face was perpetually flushed. In fact, in all the years since Bobby Hertz's first attempt, only once did the gag actually work. That was with Janie Thompson and Rick Mastro in the second half of *The Godfather: Part II.* Of course, Mastro had the fact that they were newlyweds, and that he was ten years the senior to the other boys, on his side.

Marry Dugan met her first husband while buying tickets for *Harvey*; where she became Marry Dugan Smith. She met her second husband when she was getting more popcorn during the intermission for *Cleopatra* and was ultimately left with the name Marry Dugan Davies. And she met her third husband when walking out of *Love Story*, which she'd gone to watch alone for the sixth time, and came home with the name Marry Dugan Davies-Hynde.

"Stitch" Wilkins died in the lobby after taking his grandson to see *It's a Mad, Mad, Mad, Mad World.* A heart attack crept up on him slowly throughout the second and third acts, striking like a black mamba as they shuffled out of the theater.

Morgan Sellers asked his girlfriend Josephine to marry him at the top of the stairs as they gazed over the people pulsing in and out of The Grand. He was on one knee holding the diamond up with pride as pudgy Hodgey Thurston came rumbling up the stairs, barely brushing the boy with his girth, sending Morgan down twenty-five stairs to the first landing. Morgan broke his back and never walked again. Josephine married him nonetheless. And in The Grand wouldn't you know. Hodgey paid for the entire ceremony and honeymoon out of the immense sense of guilt and responsibility he'd assumed over his part in the incident.

Smiles and tears, laughter and heartbreak vibrated in these walls. Elmore watched from his tiny booth as the town grew and changed around him.

And as Blisterwood changed, the life that passed through The Grand was inexorably absorbed by the padded walls, the velvet curtains, and the gold inlay. No major esthetic differences changed from the opening day in '28 to how it looked fifty years later, but now the transformation was clear as day. Life hung on the walls, happily cultivating more verve;

the only man taking note being the soul who'd spent his entire existence there.

But even Elmore was unaware of the cognizant recognition The Grand held for the mortal coil scuffling around her tiled floors.

He tossed the box of donuts on a side table for him to graze on throughout the long day. The projection booth was a single c-shaped hall with minute windows spaced every few feet. It was populated by double-layered, flatbed film trees and the *click*, *click*, *clicking* of the projectors. Each projector was sectioned off in its own little pool of light that diffused and disappeared in the dim calmness of the hall's abyss. On each tree sat a reel of film on its side, and the film stretched to the projector like a high arching mountain peak and through a roller, before it plummeted down to be fed into the machine. It snaked up, down, up, clasp, up, bubble out, then fastened to the bottom where it fed to the lower flatbeds, collecting itself, ready to go for the next showing.

Elmore lumbered from projector to projector, setting them up in this fashion until they were all ready to go. It took him all of fifteen minutes as he grabbed another donut, chocolate with butterscotch filling. Slowly but surely, the rest of the theater's crew wandered in, setting up for their first day in the all-new MegaPix Six.

The day's first batch of kernels popped, singing throughout the foyer.

He tinkered in the corner at his workstation, slicing fragments of story into a larger, completed films.

His alarm went off, and he shifted his rolling chair over to projector six, spattered with sticky notes. One adding two additional sixes to the number. Another above the start switch read, "Must turn off and on twice for ten seconds before starting."

Six had always been a pain. It ate more prints and possessed more idiosyncrasies than any machine was rightly allowed. But every time Elmore replaced six, the same problems reoccurred.

"Time we get this day rolling, Lucifer. Wha'd ya say?" He double and triple checked his flawless work. He flipped the switch for the light bulb, waited ten seconds, powered it down, then flipped it back on.

Elmore peeked through the port-o-hole to find a modicum crowd of nine people. The early matinee shows were the least populated.

He started the projector, and the film followed its path up and down with speed and precision. Elmore pulled the blackout lens, and the movie flashed its images on the large white screen across the room. The lights in the theater dimmed.

Steps echoed their way down the hall behind him.

In the light of the short hall leading to the projection booth stood Hal Anderson, the newly appointed manager from MegaPix. Balding with a few pathetic strands of hair plastered to his scalp in a comb-over, Hal didn't wear the burlap shirt the rest of the crew wore. He wore a shitty, black-cotton-blend button-up shirt, the logo for MegaPix embroidered above the heart.

On either side of him stood two men. One was hefty and bulging out of his flannel. He wore blue jeans and neglected work boots. The other was a young teen in the same uniform as Elmore. His face was riddled with zits and scabs, his red hair cropped in a buzz, and he wore an apathetic look of distain on his thick lips and vacant eyes. His right ear was strangely misshapen, had swelled and never quite healed right. An odd crescent line ran along the inflammation.

"Elmo, Elmo. Where the hell did that old codger—Ah, Elmo. There you are. Hard to see in this light." He carried an air of a man who believed himself to be the most important wheel in a much larger engine.

"It's Elmore, sir."

"What? Oh. Isn't that what I said? Who really cares? Not. What's. Important. Let me introduce you to a couple of grade-A guys." He motioned to the fat man in the Paul Bunyan outfit. "This here is Allan. He's here to remove the *film* projectors and replace them with the digital ones. He won't get in the way, I'm sure. Al, if you could go over to number one and start that way around."

The colossal workman thudded off to the darkened end of the booth, dragging his clanging tools with him.

"And here we have Jake, whose father has asked me to find his son a job here at MegaPix." He leaned in to whisper to Elmore but didn't lower his tone. "He isn't the most personable kid, so I figured I'd send him up here. You know, keep him away from the customers."

Elmore remembered when getting assigned to the projection booth was the highest honor a lobby-boy could hope to strive for. MegaPix used these days for public relations purposes.

Hal leaned back and slapped Jake on the back.

"Jake, this is Elmo. He's been doing projection here since before you were born. He used to all the old film-fed machines. But since we're transitioning to digital, I want you to shadow Allan as he installs the new projectors. Once he's told you everything you need to know, hang out here with Elmo and see if there's anything he can teach you. We're gonna keep a film projector, just in case, so have him show you what to do. You're gonna replace him when he's gone."

He nodded awkwardly and snuck back down the hall, out into the lobby.

Jake gave Elmore a reverse nod of recognition, glaring around the room like he was sizing up the joint, then skulked off to find Allan.

This kid didn't want to be here, didn't want to be anywhere there wasn't a joint and a game console.

When Elmore was first introduced to the booth, Todd Harken operated it through the change from Vaudeville to Film. He showed Elmore all the intricacies it took to build a reel-to-reel movie. He taught young Elmore how to splice, build, and break down a movie. Showed him what to do in case there were a jam, or if the film tangled in the flatbed. Showed him how to replace an old bulb—safely. Even how the old machines differed from the new ones, but how, in the end, they were still machines.

Something a man built and could put his hands on to fix. Like a car or a sink or a radiator.

Things built with the knowledge that everything breaks down eventually and designed so a man could remedy the situation, unlike these digital projectors that were simply giant single-use computers.

They didn't want to teach this kid what to do when it broke down. They wanted him to call a number and have someone else come out. To do what? Reboot it? It took six hours for these things to warm up and another hour to reset its programing.

With film, Elmore could fix most problems before the audience knew there was one. Once, during a showing of *The Conversation*, he saw a knot in the film, seconds away from being fed into the machine. Elmore untangled the film, and the show went on completely undisturbed.

An alarm sounded in congruence with a flashing red light on six. Elmore hurried back down the booth and booted Lucifer on the spot labeled, "Kick Here." The light and alarm settled, and everything went back to normal.

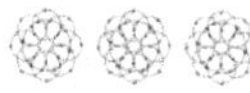

About an hour into his training, Jake annoyed Allan so profusely, his face glowed red. His large steps thudded around the corner as Elmore prepared projector five.

The large man steamed, almost literally. He pulled Jake by the collar and tossed him like a sack of potatoes at the old man.

"You take 'em. I hear one more snot-nosed remark out this kid, and I'll need to go back to anger management." His deep voice full of bass.

"Whatever." Jake straightened himself out and settled into Elmore's desk chair as the behemoth stomped back into the shadows.

Elmore finished checking the projector and hit the button to set the movie on its way. He lightly patted the machine. "That's the last one you'll ever play, Vera. Wish it could have been something better than a damn *Smurfs* sequel."

Jake squinted in his familiar distain. "Did you just call that thing *Vera*?"

Elmore approached the boy. "It's not a thing. It's a projector. And, yes, I named it Vera."

"That's fucking weird. So, what, do you like sit up here and have conversations with these *things*?" This time it was clear to Elmore he'd used the word deliberately.

“Only when I’m working on ‘em. You spend forty years up here on your own, you develop a kind of rapport with these guys. You learn their idiosyncrasies, their strengths, their weaknesses. After a while, they don’t seem all that much different from people. So, is it weird? Sure. But these projectors are as good of friends as I got.” He’d long thought of them as loved ones, proud of all they’d accomplished together.

“So, Vera’s your girlfriend, huh? Bet you sit up here alone and hump the thing when nobody’s looking.” He leaned back in Elmore’s chair, sly grin stretched across his face.

Elmore imagined slapping the kid upside the head but pretended not to hear him, choosing to work on breaking down a print.

“That’s it, isn’t it? You just sit up here all day with your meat in your hand jerking it all over these *things*. Probably jizzed on everything up here.” He considered the chair and shot out of the seat. “Oh gross, that’s probably your jerk-off chair.”

Elmore possessed no dignified response to the boy’s insolence, and he took his seat back. “Thank you.”

When he really wanted to get back at someone, being nice merely made them more upset.

He grabbed a reel and laced it on a smaller, motorized one. He turned a knob and the film fed itself from larger reel to smaller, zipping by as Elmore lightly pinched the film with his thumb and index fingers. Halting the acceleration, he fit the cells into the splicer and cut it down the break line where it was once taped together. He wound up the smaller reel and replaced it with another, repeating the process.

Elmore operated seamlessly. As if he knew the exact frame to cut on without really having to think about it.

Jake meandered around the dark space, looking at the walls covered in old movie posters, some beginning to wear and fray at the edges. “You watch all of these?”

“Every last one. It’s been a tradition of mine since I started to put the posters up here in the booth when they retire.” He glanced at the boy, hardly paying attention to the film sweeping past his fingers, and without paying it any attention, he sliced and discarded the smaller reel. “Can’t really see it in the dark, but the whole room is full of 'em. Ceiling, too."

Jake looked closer, above him a mishmash of a hundred placards all plastered on top of one another. "*Reservoir Dogs*. Cool. The part where he cuts the dude's ear off is disgusting."

"Speaking of ears." Elmore nodded toward Jake's engorged ear.

Jake covered it, embarrassed. "Oh, this?"

"Mind me asking what happened?"

"This punk-freak-loser, Bass Harper, attacked me and my boys at the homecoming dance last year. Bit the thing right off. They were able to sew it back on, but it hasn't looked the same since."

Elmore's stomach churned at the thought. All he could do was nod again, raising his eyebrows sympathetically. School really had changed since his days at Blisterwood High.

"It's cool. Fucker got expelled for the year. Not to mention, we kicked the shit out of him at the dance. Son of a bitch came back though. And he's huge. Like *retardedly* big."

Elmore didn't know what to say, so they fell back into a long silence.

Elmore tore down the film, dropping the excess remnants in a tiny pile on the ground.

Jake studying the posters in the darkness.

"I'll be honest. I don't really like movies. Gaming is more my thing. Movies are so…boring."

This last comment was a shot to Elmore's pride. *Make fun of me all you want, but go after my friends, and I take offense.*

"I mean they can be fun, sometimes. But on a whole, I'd rather be playing my PlayStation. Movies, there's nothing going on. You're just sitting there. Blah. At least with gaming, you feel like you're accomplishing something."

Elmore engaged the brat and spun his chair out to face him. "You telling me, you never seen a movie that made you feel something? You never been scared of the zombies, or laughed so hard you choked on your popcorn? You'd rather sit there playing the same level on repeat until you beat it? Doing the same damn thing, over and over again. Yeah, sounds like an accomplishment to me."

"What do you call what you're doing? Slicing and reeling and playing the same movies all day?"

The shit had a point. "Yeah, but I get paid to do this."

"Whatever."

When Elmore was finished breaking down the print, he got projector four ready.

Jake had wandered off down the hall, playing a game on his cell phone.

"Kid, why don't you come over here and learn something."

Jake sighed and lumbered over to the projector. "What?"

"You heard Hal. They're keeping one of the projectors, just in case. You're gonna need to know how to use it, 'kay?"

"Just in case of what?"

"In case shit hits the fan and these digital suckers break down. Now, I held off threading this one, so I could show you what to do." Elmore walked around to the flatbed tree and pulled the end of the film out from the spot where it was neatly tucked away. "You start by taking the tail end here and feeding it through these wheels here, called the brain. Then, you take the tail, stringing it up through these rollers, like so."

He stretched the film out and ran it through a couple of rollers that were bolted to the ceiling amongst the posters.

"You then take the tail and bring it through the projector itself."

Around the projector on its right side, he opened a network of gears and clamps. "You take the tail and fit it into these clamps here."

Jake was playing his game again.

Elmore slapped it out of Jake's hand with a *thwack*. "Pay attention."

"Hey, *fucker*." He checked the phone for any cracks as if inspecting a valuable crystal. "If you broke it, you're buying me a new one."

"I'm not doing this for my health, kid. This is gonna be up to you when I'm gone. You better get the hang of it, or you're not gonna have a job for very long."

"Fuck you, man. Don't you touch my phone. I don't care if you're old. I'll kick your ass." Elmore saw he'd rattled the little shit, which gave him an immense surge of joy.

"Put the damn phone away and pay attention. Now, as I was saying, you take the tail and fit it into these clamps here." He stretched the film out further, slamming clamps shut. "You need to make sure you get the film to line up with these little teeth here. See?"

Jake looked at the machine defiantly. His scowl making Elmore wonder if he was actually paying attention or simply brooding about his stupid phone. "See?"

"Jesus. Yeah, I see."

"'Kay. Now, this here lens is where the light comes through. It's extremely hot. You never want to touch it. If the film jams, depending on the print, it can set it on fire. That's why I'm being such a stickler. You gotta get it right, or the cost of the print is gonna come out of yer pay."

Jake perked up and took a closer interest.

"Yeah, thought that might get you. Now, once we feed the tail past the lens, we've got a bunch more wheels and clamps to put it through." He pulled the film down to the bottom of the projector with another network of machinery, including a tiny, red light. He strung it through, up, around, over, under, with Jake paying much closer attention.

"Now you see this red light here? That's the laser that reads the soundtrack. We gotta line it up just right, or the sound'll be off and all stretched out." He fit the film into place and closed another fastener.

"Next, you gotta bubble out the film. Most people use three fingers, but my hands are old and puffy, so I just use two." He wrapped the film around his first two fingers on his left hand then fed them onto a roller with more teeth. "Next, you take the rest of the film here and feed it through these wheels here. You gotta get them right, 'cause they keep the tension on the film."

The film slid through a series of rollers, up, down, up, down. Elmore walked back around the projector to the tree, extending it to the bottom flatbed where a metal ring was fit into the center.

"Finally, you take the tail, pinch it, and fit it into this ring here, where it collects the film again. Got it?"

Jake had his phone out again.

"Goddamn it. What'd I say about that phone?" He took another swipe at it, but Jake moved it out of the way before the old man could make contact. "Put it away."

"Christ, you old coot. I got a text from my girlfriend. Chill."

"I'll chill when I know you understand this machine backwards and forwards."

"I saw. You loop it around the spinners there, and then you pinch it off in that giant-sized cock ring down there. I'm not a fucking idiot. A monkey could do this job."

The words sank into Elmore like venom. He was losing his temper.

"Let me see you do it then." He undid his work, one roller or clamp at a time back to where he'd started.

Jake wore a vacant expression, mouth agape, as he stared at the projector and film tree. Paralyzed.

"Looks like someone's not as smart as a monkey."

"*Pff*. I got it." Jake grabbed the tail at the center of the print and stared at the brain, unsure of where to start. "Maybe you could show me one more time."

"Thought so."

It took three tries, but finally, Jake caught on once he'd pocketed his phone and actually concentrated. When Jake finished, his bubble was a bit too large at the bottom and the teeth didn't match up with the holes on the film stock, but all in all, the kid was retaining what Elmore taught him.

Fixing Jake's mistakes, Elmore closed the projector. "Good. Starting to get the hang of it. Now, last but not least, ya turn the sucker on."

He glanced at his watch.

"Right…about…now." He hit a large red plastic button on the side and the whole thing went into production.

A dopey grin sprouted amongst the field of zits on Jake's face. When Todd Harken taught him, he, too, had felt the astonishment, knowing he'd made the machine work. "Pretty neat, eh?"

The goofy smile on Jake's face slipped away and fell back into his general apathy. "Whatever. Like I said, a monkey could do it."

"Ack." Elmore waved his hand in dismissal, lumbered back to his desk, and tore down more prints.

"What do you call this one? Lola?"

"That one there is Mike. Hardly ever had a glitch. Hence, why I taught you on him. Do me a favor and go get me a cup of soda, would you? All this indifference is making me thirsty." Anything to get the little prick out of his hair.

"If it gets me out of this fire hazard, sure." Jake took off down the dark hall to the spiral staircase leading to the concessions.

"And don't spit in it. I've got a sixth sense for detecting all forms of bodily secretions."

Jake raised his hand in acknowledgment then flicked the old man the bird.

"I saw that."

By midday, Allan was done replacing projectors one, three, and five. Hal was strategic about which theaters would be rendered useless for the few hours it took to boot the digital ones.

The projection booth was split into two levels, one through three on the bottom, four through six on top. Projectors one and three were chosen because of the ease in transporting the new equipment. The larger theaters were on the top level, so it simply made more sense to keep those ones operational for as long as possible.

MegaPix was interested in one thing: money.

More people could fit in the larger theaters, which meant more money for MegaPix, which meant a fraction of a percentage boost in the quarterly dividends for the shareholders at BigCorp.

Over the years, The Grand had gone through various retrofittings and remodels. In the 50's, the theater was split from an enormous single theater to the upstairs and down stairs. Todd Harken put up an amazing stink with the owners back then. He even threatened to quit his job, but soon realized Elmore would take over, so he backed down.

In the early '80s, with the advent of the new big blockbusters like *Jaws, The Godfather*, and *Star Wars*, the new owners decided to remodel again and split the upstairs into the existing six total theaters. It was Elmore's opportunity to mount the complaints, but ultimately lost the argument and almost his job as well.

But the remodels were always aware of the history in The Grand, and if anything, they reupholstered and deep cleaned the facilities. The history was what gave the place its charm, and the rotating owners were never too blind to realize that.

However, when MegaPix bought the Old Lady a few months back, Elmore was too old and too tired to fight.

Lacking any true protégé forced him to stay on until they could find a replacement. Without anyone young enough or who cared enough to fight the changes, without as much as a raised eyebrow, The Grand was gutted. The sole portion that remained untouched was the double-layered projection booth. And with the MegaPix standards and protocols, that, too, was set to be modernized eventually. Changing out the projectors was simply the first step in the process.

Elmore set up projector two, Johnny, for the last time while Jake sat texting his girlfriend, doing a piss poor job at feigning interest. Elmore slammed Johnny's side door shut and without looking at his watch this time, hit the red start button on the side. As soon as the film was finished, Allan would break Johnny down and replace him with a giant box.

Elmore said goodbye to an old friend on his deathbed. He blinked back tears but was too stifled by the boy in the corner and the task at hand to allow himself to cry.

"It's so dark up here," Jake said, more than a hint of whine in his voice. "Don't you ever miss the sun?"

"You get used to it. It's not easy, I'll admit. But that's why this job isn't for everybody. You need to be a special breed—"

"Yeah, sure. Listen, I gotta go make a call. These things are too loud. Is there someplace I can go that's quiet?" Jake held out his phone as if to prove his need.

"You could go to Hal's office and ask him if you could use his phone. Usually pretty quiet in there." Elmore got the reaction he wanted when Jake's zit-clustered face scrunched up, realizing what the old man was really saying.

"Whatever. I think I saw a door over here." He took off down the dark hall and around the corner. *What if he finds the door?*

"*No*." Elmore hurried behind.

Around the corner, next to where projector one—Sally—a door hid in the wall that blended with the medley of movie posters. If you weren't looking closely, you'd never notice it was there.

"What? Is this where you keep the bodies?"

Jake was inside before Elmore even rounded the corner.

"This room is private. I can't have you in here," he said when he finally caught up.

"Where's the damn light switch? Why is it so fucking cold?" Jake felt around in the dark, finding the switch and filling the room with a sudden and brazen light that blinded Elmore for an instant.

The minute alcove was filled with gray metal racks of canned reels. Stacks of film lie on top of one another, crowding the room so one could hardly walk.

"You need to go. This room is restricted access."

Jake carefully wandered amongst the racks. "What is all this stuff?"

"My personal collection."

"Like they're stolen?"

"No. *Repurposed.* When the theater breaks down a print, they send it back to the studio for disposal. Sometimes, they send more than one print. If it's a movie worth keeping, I simply flub the numbers, tell them there was an accident, and only send them back the original print. Todd Harken, my mentor, started it when he worked here. The films in here are extremely delicate. They need to be kept in a dry room that is cold enough to maintain them. You shouldn't be in here." Elmore panicked, with a hot flush that probably matched the embroidered MegaPix logo on his shirt.

"I'm not gonna hurt anything, old man. Don't worry. Just wanna take a look at what you've got here."

Jake scanned the titles written in a clear print along the edges of the canisters in masking tape. *Metropolis, Wings, All*

Quiet on the Western Front, The Love Parade, Cimarron, Cavalcade, A Farewell to Arms, She Done Him Wrong, It Happened One Night, The Thin Man, and *Mutiny on the Bounty.* "How are these arranged? I've never heard of any of them?"

"Chronologically. They're old, that's why. Those date back to '27. Got a couple around here older than that. Lots of Chaplin and Keaton. Baby Peggy. Rudy Valentino. You even know what I'm talking about, or is this all Greek, kid?" A wash of pride rest in Elmore as he listed the names of his old friends.

"As in Charlie Chaplin? Like silent? Damn, this shit is old. Why'd you want to keep this crap around? It's outdated garbage."

His words singed Elmore's pride.

"None of you young people give a damn about history, do you?" He rushed in and shoved Jake out.

Jake twisted, pointing to the corner, at something covered in a sheet, that caught his attention. "What's that?"

The boy broke free of Elmore's grip, past the stacks of film canisters to the gigantic, dusty purple sheet. Jake grabbed one end and pulled on it hard, kicking up a cloud of once-settled soot.

They coughed and swatted the dust clear to reveal a giant wooden box with what looked like a million black and white keys.

"Is that an organ?"

"A Mighty Wurlitzer to be exact."

"I swear to God, you are the weirdest old man I've ever met. *Why* do you have a freaking organ in here?" Jake's contempt exaggerated his usual expression.

"Back when The Grand played silent films, there used to be a full orchestra to play along with the movies. They were as requisite to the experience as the film itself. But over time, the musicians got to be too expensive, so the owners filled the bill and got the organ. This puppy can do everything a full orchestra can do, and you only needed to pay one man. I call him Chester."

"You and these fucking names. Can you play it? Looks like the cockpit of a spaceship." Jake leaned in closer.

"I could, if it was still set up. The pipes and whatnot were all taken out to make room for the new theaters."

"Cool. My grandpa played the organ at his church. Used to play for me when he was still alive." Jake's venom made way for a sad downturn of his mouth and eyes.

"You close to your grandpa?"

"Taught me everything when I was a kid, so yeah. Basically raised me while my parents were at work." As though recognizing his own humanity, his face flushed, and he spat, "Don't think you're gonna use that against me, old man. He could be a real bastard sometimes."

Jake hurried out to the dark hall and the projectors. Elmore replaced the sheet over the organ, and taking a last look at the room, turned out the light and closed the door.

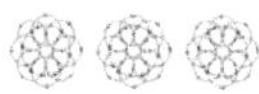

By ten o'clock, the last show was in progress on the new, digital beast taking over theater four. Elmore broke down more film to send back to the studios, where they would be destroyed. It always seemed like such a ridiculous extra step to the old man, but it was the way things worked, so he went along with it. Hal had long left for the day, braving the six o'clock traffic on Main Street back to his home in Highland Gardens five towns away.

Elmore was to show Jake how to shut down the theater for the night. Yet, as much as he enjoyed the silence, Elmore had not seen the boy in over two hours.

He finished tearing the film into its shorter sections and descended the spiral iron stairs to look for Jake. The concession area's popcorn machine had long popped its last kernel for the day. In the main lobby, the ushers did their last sweep with their push brooms.

"You seen Jake around?"

"Who?"

"Snot-nosed punk, vacant stare, pock marks like the lunar surface."

"Gonna have to be more specific than that, buddy." The middle-aged man's body jiggled as he chuckled at his own quip.

"Thinks he's gonna take over my booth because his daddy knows Hal."

"Oh. Yeah. Shit heel. Out back doing God knows what."

A pounding came from the front door. Elmore opened them for a young beefy giant in a long coat and enormous, black work boots. He had sunken eyes and a paler complexion than Elmore.

"What can I do you for, son? Last movie just started. Afraid we're shutting down for the night."

"One," he forced out in an unsettling grunt.

"You sure, trailers are done, and the movie's already ten minutes in."

"One…please." His voice was like chains on gravel.

"If you say so. Eight fifty. Afraid the concessions are all shut down."

The giant handed over a wad of cash.

"Theater four. Up the stairs and to the right."

The colossus thanked him and skulked off up the stairs as Elmore relocked the front doors.

The usher scurried over. "Hey, you know who that was, right?"

"Not a clue." *Does it matter?*

"That was Bass Harper. He's been All State defensive linemen for the past two years. Singlehandedly crippled the quarterback at Evergreen."

The name shot in Elmore's memory: the conversation with Jake about his ear. "Can't say I've heard of him. Don't follow sports much."

When Elmore opened up the back door, he found Jake and a doughy-faced girl sitting on some crates, smoking a joint. When their glazed-over gazes detected Elmore, they instinctively hid the joint behind their backs, falling suspiciously silent.

"Kid, smoke break is up. Let's go. Gotta show you how to shut this place down." Something Elmore said must have been funny, he figured, because the two teens started barking erratic laughs. "C'mon. Your girly friend'll have to stay here."

They laughed louder.

"Fuck it." Elmore huffed back to the projector booth.

Let that punk find his old ear-biting buddy down here then.

After ten minutes, Jake made his way up the spiral staircase, the girl in tow. They seemed to navigate each step like it was a greater hurdle than the last.

"She can't be up here." In all his years, Elmore had permitted only one person up to the booth. A girl named Janice Watkins, a date he'd hoped to impress as they watched *Love Story*. She gave him a peck at the end of the night but never returned another call.

"Chill, Elmo. Tina wants to go to film school. She's actually interested in this shit for some reason." The girl gave him a light back-handed slap to the chest.

"Jake was telling me you've got a secret stash of films. I was wondering if I could take a look." Her voice was sweet but lethargic. Her long bangs covered most of her dark-circled eyes, and her bushy hair reminded him of Peg from *Lady and the Tramp*.

"That was not a secret for Jake to tell ya, missy. Sorry, they're real delicate, and you're not supposed to be up here in the first place."

"Please? Do you have any Kubrick? He's my all-time favorite. I'm writing a paper on him for my AP English class over the summer."

Elmore worshipped the great Stanley Kubrick and his full command of everything—the mise en scene, the names of the characters, the subtle hints of his own personal psychology revealed over the litany of his entire works. Elmore loved every detail of every movie.

"What's your favorite?"

"The correct answer here is *Barry Lyndon*, but I'd be lying if I didn't say *2001*."

"Interesting. Jake where you been keeping this one? Wish I could pass this place on to her instead of you. At least she knows what she's talking about. You're right, missy. *Barry Lyndon* is the hidden masterpiece in the Kubrick catalog. The only one to get five stars at the Kubrick film festival a few years back. But *2001* was his game changer." Elmore sat back and contemplated them. "Jake, how'd you and your girly friend like to have a private screening. We'll have to use ole Lucifer. But I think we can get by."

"Oh, please. That would be so much fun." Tina's eyes lit up, exposing how bloodshot they really were. She kissed Jake on the cheek.

"Yeah, sure. Why not? I ain't got shit to do tonight."

Elmore led the teens to the hidden closet and revealed his buried treasure. Tina rushed in, jaw ajar, while Jake waited outside.

"Wow. How many do you have in here?"

"Don't know exactly. Over three fifty, I know that." He walked over to a row of films from 1973.

"Wait a second. *Clockwork* came out in '71, and *Lyndon* came out in '75. Kubrick didn't have any films in 1973." Tina's face was a ball of confusion, straining desperately to calculate through her marijuana haze.

"None that were released." Elmore's face grew into a thin, sly smile.

"What? I don't follow."

"It's widely known that Mr. Kubrick was obsessed with the life and times of Napoleon. He actually was planning a biopic as his next film after *Clockwork Orange*. Unfortunately, he was forced to scrap the project when it soared over budget and over schedule. Much of what eventually became *Barry Lyndon* actually came out of the film he was making about Napoleon." Pride puffed his chest, like he'd won an unspoken game. Triumph.

"And you're saying this is the Napoleon movie?"

Elmore's smirk spoke for itself.

"Holy shit. How many people have ever seen this?"

"Maybe ten in the whole world know it exists. I haven't even seen it. Don't know if it's any good."

"Of course, it's good. It's Kubrick."

"Been waiting for a special occasion. Seeing as I'm leaving soon, I figured why not give it a whirl?"

"Aw man, do we have to? I fucking hate history. Can't we at least watch a movie with explosions and fighting?" Jake chimed from out in the hall.

"Ever hear of Waterloo, kid? This'll have plenty of violence. I assure you." Elmore's eyebrows jumped and his nose flared.

"Fine. But if this movie blows, I'm telling Hal about your stash."

"That's a wager I'm willing to risk."

Elmore pulled out the six separate reels that made up the Napoleon film as Tina settled into her seat in the middle of the theater. He'd made Jake stay behind to thread the movie in Lucifer.

"You need to learn how to deal with the old bastard, considering he's gonna be the sole film projector on hand. Cantankerous *sonofabitch*."

There was a check list of extra steps one needed to know in order to operate Lucifer, and Elmore was more than thorough in his explanation of each one. But, due to a mixture of his hormones and teenage angst, Jake heard maybe every third word.

When the last clamp was shut, the left corner kicked three times, the start button punched in exactly the right configuration—"Shave and a Haircut" of all things, and the carriage containing the bulb cooled by the jimmy-rigged portable fan, everything was set to go, and Elmore let the boy return to his girlfriend in theater six.

The movie jumped right into the opening credits with a loud orchestral boom that sounded hauntingly familiar from the *Lyndon* score. Elmore hadn't found the time to splice all the reels together, so he was going to do it old school, the way he and Todd Harken did it in the good old days. He'd have to splice them as they came along, one reel ending and feeding into another. This didn't bother Elmore in the least, considering he'd be watching the movie from the port-o-hole the entire time anyway.

It began on a battlefield in the French countryside as cannon balls whizzed through the air, exploding into the grounds of a farmhouse, throwing soldiers and peasants alike in their concussive blasts. Elmore popped his head through the tiny window and shouted over the movie, "What'd I tell ya, kid? Plenty of violence."

Jake twisted in his seat and waved at Elmore to get lost as he settled back into his girlfriend.

Elmore sat back down, a grin splitting his face. "I can already tell this is going to be one *hell-of-a* movie."

But as the movie dragged on, it grew clear why the project had been abandoned. Slow, convoluted, and full of melodramatic silence, all of which created a draining effect on the old man who had been up since early that morning. His eyelids grew heavy, and he nearly missed the transition between the second and third reels.

Shortly thereafter, Elmore, weary from a day of heartbreak and pubescent arguing, finally succumbed to sleep during a scene in which Josephine dropped her bodice and stood in a great room of Versailles stark naked in front of a grubby and rotund Napoleon.

Jake took this sudden influx of nudity and romance in the story to sneak a groping of Tina's left breast. She swatted his hand away, stealing a glance at the booth.

The old man leaned against the glass, asleep, and she let Jake continue, starting for his zipper and pressing her mouth and tongue to his.

Bass entered the theater from the back entrance. The explosions of cannon fodder masked his hulking steps, a large double-sided battle-axe in hand. Not until he raised the axe did either of them caught the shadow on the obstructed silver screen.

The double-crescent silhouette turned them around to find a loose and demonic glare.

The axe came down, singing through the air, before the blade landed perfectly between the two teens, who bolted in opposite directions.

Bass struggled to relieve the blade from the metal and plastic armrest, frustrated, broken, and unhinged.

The teens screamed from the foot of the theater, yet Elmore slept on, unable to distinguish the racket from the battle scene explosions. Reel three was near its end, old and weathered as it was, and the teeth snagged it in one of the spinning wheels of the projector.

A frame of a bloodied soldier, screaming on the war-torn field was frozen on screen for a moment, which soon faded to a red-brown umber, showing the grain in the old film stock, before bubbling and quickly catching fire.

Flames spread rapidly along the strip, draped across the room as per the old way of projecting movies, catching on the scraps of film at the foot of Elmore's desk and eventually on the poster-covered walls and ceiling.

The sprinklers were tripped on, but the water lines hadn't been set up yet, a detail Hal had paid the city inspector to overlook.

Plumes of rusty gas from the old pipes filled The Grand, making it all the more difficult to see.

By the time Elmore woke up, the whole of the booth blazed like a golden ocean in the middle of a squall.

Smoke burned Elmore's eyes and choked his lungs as he fell from his stool near the port-o-hole.

The air was easier to breathe on the ground, but fear petrified Elmore. He crawled to the spiral stairs, where he skidded down, tumbling over himself and landing on the tile below, knocked out cold.

In the theater, Bass freed his axe from the armrest, and stepping over entire rows of seats, chased after the two screaming youths.

Jake and Tina pulled on the exit door, but it was jammed.

The flames from the booth crept into theater six, where the synthetic noise-reducing foam on the walls caught quick.

Bass jumped over the last three rows, landing with a ground-shaking thud. The monumental beast of a man hurried for the exit tunnel, but because it was sized for moviegoers of average height, he was forced to crouch, slowing his pursuit.

Jake gave the door a desperate tug and freed it from its jam.

A plastic broom and dustpan, now broken in halves on the ground, had been slung across two outside door handles to trap them inside.

Jake and Tina hurried into the lobby, down the large curving staircase, to the front entrance, but the doors were locked.

They screamed as the giant emerged from the theater hallway, smoke billowing out around him.

The fire spread to the other theaters, igniting The Grand like a furnace, and everything MegaPix did to give the Old Lady a facelift melted away like the Wicked Witch in a water park.

Jake and Tina cut across the floor, past the concession stand to the back, only to find a collapsed ceiling brightly blocking their sole way out.

A strip of florescent lights came loose from the ceiling, swinging down and knocking Tina to the ground. The glass from the light burst, and a large shard swiped past Jake's face, cutting off the distorted end of his ear once more.

The rest of the ceiling came crashing down around Jake, pinning him to the tile floor, unconscious.

The upper balcony weakened under Bass's over-sized feet, his axe now holstered on his back. As his prey rushed under him and out of sight, an explosion of flame rumbled out from where they'd gone.

The flames did his job for him, so Bass turned back to the smoke piping around the edges of the hidden door.

He ripped it open and found the kind man who'd let him in earlier passed out at the foot of an iron spiral staircase.

He hadn't done anything wrong. He didn't deserve this fate.

Bass carried the old man from the stairwell back to the balcony. The curved stairs along the sides of the lobby now fully ablaze. There was no getting down them. Bass, on impulse, leapt from the landing. The balcony collapsed behind them, along with it most of theaters four, five, and six.

The Old Lady had taken enough.

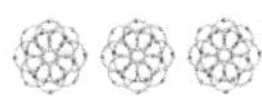

When Elmore finally came to, he found himself coughing on the doughnut shop's curb across the street.

The place he'd worked his entire life was lit up, smoke staining the night sky. Flames devoured the large pillar resting on top of The Grand.

As he stood, something soft formed in his hand, the red bowtie, singed at the corners. A parting gift, bequeathed to him by the only love he'd ever known.

He searched Main Street, confused as to how he made it out alive. In the shadows of the alley, he caught Bass Harper's glowing sunken gaze before the giant slipped away, dissolving into the shadows.

Elmore stared, struggling to reconcile the disappointment of the lost Kubrick film.

The marquee tumbled to the ground.

"What a shame." Elmore began his long walk home down Main Street.

VI.

Many in Green Valley believe that on the day Jinx Jenkins arrived in the valley, a great shockwave of calamity spread throughout the county. Though no one knows the precise date this occurred, the event has been attributed to such catastrophes as the Élan river catching fire, the destruction of The Grand theater, and even the disaster at the Swingo Candy factory, which forever left the valley in a continual layer of gray-green filth.

Undoubtedly, his appearance became a scapegoat for many in the valley to explain their own misgivings: A lost job, a stain on one's last clean tie, a failing grade on a test.

Some of the citizenship were affected personally; none more famous than that of Old Lady Foster. For on the night before Ms. Foster was scheduled to give birth, Jinx passed her house, acknowledging her presence in the window with a nod, and kept on his way.

MILLENNIAL

Once, a poor, old woman lived in the foothills of Green Valley. Made old by the circumstances of her life. Mary Foster was known the county over as The Human Incubator, as she had been pregnant for the last 257 months.

Her pregnancy went as any pregnancy might. She received regular ultrasounds, took vitamins, and kept away from cigarettes and alcohol—save the occasional glass of wine.

Everything appeared to be right on schedule until her due date. Yet the baby never came. The doctors told her to be patient because these things sometimes happen.

So, she waited.

But the baby never came. When seven days passed without any change, the doctors decided to induce. To their surprise, the child held tight. The only course of action was to retrieve the child through C-section. The doctors put Mary under and sliced her open. The lead surgeon put his hands inside and was shocked to feel a bite.

A tiny hand came out and extended a middle finger.

The doctors had a single option: sew Mary back up. The child did not wish to be born. And so, the baby never came.

Holidays passed, children grew tall and strong, and Mary remained pregnant. Her life was thrown out of whack. And as the months and years ticked by and the child inside her grew, she found herself incapacitated. Soon, the burden grew too large for her to walk, and she needed to be wheeled around. Her diet changed, as did her bathroom schedule. She sold all of her normal clothes and spent a fortune on muumuus—the only thing that fit her belly. But worst of all, consumed with pain, she hardly attained a few hours of broken sleep each night. Mary was forced to move in to a nursing home where they tended to her needs.

The father was a one-night stand, a passing traveler on his way out west. She'd never got his name, let alone a number to reach him, but he might as well have not existed at all. Nonetheless, Mary habitually pictured and cursed his face. After a while, though, even his face faded, and she was left with a melting pot of emotions. Hatred and fear and anxiety and discomfort and frustration and happiness and love and lots and lots of pain.

At first, she referred to the baby as It. But after a while, Mary saw fit to give the child a name, so she called him Junior.

Junior aged within Mary, siphoning away her youth. Middle age brought her liver spots and wrinkles. Her skin grew thin and her eyes weary.

Hope had left her.

When the last drop of life was suckled and nothing was left for Junior to reap, the baby finally came. Fully grown with teeth and hair and a beard, Mary awoke one morning to find Junior at the foot of her bed. Despite his appearance, he had the mental capacity of an infant.

Mary spoon-fed him, scooping up the spittle and shoveling it back into his man-sized mouth. She changed his diapers and clothes and even gave him baths. And in spite of all her newfound hardship, Mary had never been so happy.

At last, she was able to stand and walk on her own—a thing she'd dreamt of whenever she did sleep. She could drink alcohol again. And although she never smoked cigarettes before, she started up, just because she could.

She had her body back.

Junior relied on his mother for everything. She cooked and cleaned and earned the money despite his fully capable body. For he was naïve to the ways of the world and, like any child, assumed all the world to be his juvenile right.

One day, old and withered and drained, Mary grew ill. She needed Junior to take care of her.

The man pouted and kicked and cried and cursed.

Dishes piled high, and clothes grew in heaps, soiled and stained. An odor fell about the place so foul, not even Junior could deny it.

At last, he realized the weight *he* must bear, so Junior picked up a spoon and fed his mother the way she once did for him.

He ventured out into the world and discovered, ever so harshly, that the world was not immediately his. Rather, it was up to him to earn his way and stake his claim. He found work, and in time, an appreciation for his mother took hold. Resentment gone, he realized Mary, with all her hardship, always did the best she could. And wasn't that all anyone could ever ask?

The day came when Mary finally died, old and gray with a smile on her face and Junior at her side.

VII.

Quite often, businesses are detested unanimously by the people of the communities they reside in. In Green Valley, that business was Jefferson Towing. Every day, new complaints on the company made their way to the authorities. And every day, Jefferson Towing opened back up, searching the streets for their next victims.

In a large dirt lot, right off of Jefferson Street on the outskirts of Lakeview, unclaimed cars piled high. Along the street, a tall chain-link fence with barbed wire connected to a tiny wooden shack, where casualties of the company stood before a thick pane of glass, arguing for the right to get their property back. Paper filled the cramped office—stacked and pinned to the walls. Some considered the man who worked in the office as the meanest man in all of Lakeview.

And on the day Jinx Jenkins decided to rest his weary bones in the waiting area, crouched down beneath the glass, the man did not disappoint, berating the bum and compelling him to move on with a cattle prod. Jinx stumbled to his feet and cursed the man for his cruelty. Had he known what his actions might lead to, the man might have chosen to forgo his evil ways and allow the vagrant a few minutes rest.

FUCK, PUCK

"What do we do?" For the first time all night, Puck didn't know what to say.

Feet stomped as a group of young boys hurried off toward the Taste-E-Freeze. The lone street light hung directly over the Arbor Sanctuary portal, and the drive-in movie theater sign's bulbs flashed, opposite the Taste-E-Freeze.

"He's dead."

"Yeah, I can see that, Novice."

"What the hell was he doing running in front of the car like that?"

"It's a game they play." He stood over the kid with hands on his hips.

"So, you knew they were there?"

"'Course not. What do you take me for, a murderer? I knew they *might* be there. Hoped they wouldn't." He crouched next to the body.

The boy was maybe sixteen, wearing yellow running shorts and nothing else. His body was thin and lanky, his chest still void of any hair. His dopey and foolish face said, "Ow. That hurt. Why did you hit me?"

I'd never seen anyone dead before.

Certainly never killed anyone.

The whole scene freaked me out. Most of all how calm Puck was acting.

Part of me wanted to scream.

"What do we do now?"

"Christ, Novice, calm your tits. Help me with his legs. I've got an idea."

"Calm my—*Puck*. You just killed this kid. Fucked him straight up. He's dead. No more. Gonzo. What the hell could you possibly have an idea about?" Adrenaline throbbed through me.

"Just grab his fucking legs."

My mind a fog of half thoughts and broken logic, so I helped him with the body.

His skin was still warm.

We had difficulty moving the kid—at best, he weighed a buck-fifty.

No biggie, I've lifted that.

But when you put it into the context of a human body, loose and broken, the weight gets shifted into corners you didn't realize existed.

His ass kept scraping along the asphalt.

Puck opened the back hatch, and we swung his limp limbs up and into Puck's car. He took off his hat, wiped his brow, and grabbed the delivery bag.

"I think it might be a little late to serve him a burger."

"Quiet. Help me, goddamn it." He unzipped the bag, took out the food, and replaced it with the kid, ass first.

"Whoa, hey, listen, I'm not cutting this kid up or burying him in the woods or anything. You hit the kid. I was in the passenger seat. I'm not going to jail for a delivery job, asshole." I heard the *clang* of a jail cell as I backed away with my hands in the air.

"That's not what I'm doing. Grab hold of his head and push, would you? We need to get this fucker completely inside the bag. I'm attempting to save his life."

I lifted one of the kid's hands and watched it fall. "Yup, I'm pretty sure this fucker is dead. No coming back from dead. Kind of a law of nature, if you know what I mean."

He shot knives at my face. "Grab. His. Head. Now."

I pushed, and I swear I heard the kid's neck break.

I'm going to hell. I'm going to hell. I'm going to hell.

Finally, once we'd wrangled all his limbs into the bag, Puck zipped it up and pressed buttons on the display. "Did this with a Pekinese once. Thing darted out in front of me. Couldn't stand to watch the thing die."

"And it worked?"

"Well enough. Dog didn't remember how to bark anymore, and he rolled onto his back every time he took a piss. Other than that, he seemed pretty good."

Bing.

The bag finished.

I waited, sure the bag was about to rustle.

Nothing.

Puck reached for the zipper.

The bag gave a violent shake, and we both jumped.

"Fuck, shit, cock almighty."

We waited a little longer.

Nothing.

Puck made for the zipper again.

"Dude, seriously. What if the kid is all mangled and deformed and shit? What the hell are we going to do?"

Puck waved me off and held the zipper tab in his fingers.

Did he possess the courage to open it?

"Fuck it." He undid the zipper, throwing off the top and shielding himself from what was inside.

Nothing.

A motionless bag.

Puck and I crept forward to take a peek.

There he was, the kid's face still dopey and questioning, simply a little more smushed now.

"Fuck. Kid's still dead."

He pushed his hat back on his head. "Shit. I thought for sure that was gonna work."

Suddenly, an alarm sounded. We both glanced up at the tablet on the dash. It was flashing red. The food was late. Without thinking, we both rushed back to the station wagon and hurried off to the house on Pimlington Way. The guy we gave the food to was pretty huge and mad as hell about his food being late, but he was the last thing we were concerned with.

There was a corpse in the bed of Puck's wagon, and if we didn't figure out what to do next, we were both gonna be using cigarettes as currency for the rest of our damn lives.

We both walked back to the car and sat in silence for a bit, trying to work out our next step. I was at a loss. My mind swirled, questioning if I was the kind of guy who did well in prison. From what I'd seen on TV and movies, I was pretty sure I was not.

Then, for whatever reason, Puck started belching and farting really loud. Stunk. Bad enough to water my eyes and make me want to vomit.

"Dude, do you mind?" said Puck.

"What are you talking about? That was you."

"It most certainly was not me."

Another fart sounded, and we both looked back at the body in the bag. The kids foot gave a twitch, and we bolted out of the car. Part of me was relieved we weren't going to spend the rest of our lives in the clink. But everything else in my body screamed that what I'd just seen was as far from natural as snow in summer or peanut butter and mayonnaise.

"See, Novice. Told you it would work. C'mon, help me get him out of the bag." He opened the hatch.

Hesitant, I made sure to keep my distance.

What in holy hell have we unleashed on the world?

The leg kicked in mid-air, struggling to make sense of its situation.

"Get over here and give me a hand, damn it."

I eased my way over, grabbed a limb, and we both pulled. Out came the kid, thrown from the bag. He lay in a still heap on the cement. Twisted and tied in knots, his arms, legs and neck all angled in different directions. "Fuck, we killed him *again*."

Then, the body straightened itself back out. Limb knots untied, appendages popped back into place, and its head spun around. He got to his bare feet and studied us like he'd never seen a person before.

"Jesus, kid, you okay? Scared us for a bit there." Puck approached, examining him.

Almost bird-like, he tilted his head, inquisitively regarding Puck, then let out a high-pitched, squealing fart.

"Kids a bit of a derp, if you know what I mean. Only question now is, was he a derp before or because of what we did to him?"

"Gee, Puck. I don't know. Let's ask him. Kid, were you always an idiot, or is it because we hit you with our car, you flew twenty feet, landed on asphalt—with your skull, and then were shoved into our magic bag that we're not really sure what it does?"

He opened his mouth, as if to say something, and let out a belch.

Puck pulled out a joint and a lighter.

"I said I'd never smoke while on the job. But this is different." He sparked the lighter, catching the kid's wide-eyed attention.

The kid reached for the flame.

Puck backed off, joint in his mouth.

"Fuck, derp. Give a man some space when he smokes his drugs. I mean, really."

"He's attracted to the flame."

"I see that. But can I light my jay first? Damn." He lit his joint then gave the lighter to the kid, who waited for it to light itself. When it didn't, he threw a fit.

I held his hands, placing his thumb on the flint and showed him how it worked. When he saw the flame again, his cries ceased.

The flame went out.

Right before he started up with the screams, I lit it for him.

He attempted it for himself, like a child learning to eat ice cream.

When he got it, he was stuck in the flame's trance.

I stood back and stole the joint from Puck, taking a big, long hit.

"What now?"

We didn't know what else to do, so we put the gangly derp in the back seat with all the garbage and drove off. He played with the lighter, trying to touch the flame every once and a while, only to dart his fingers back and suck on the wound. Then, he'd start up with it all over again.

The bag chimed again. *Bing.*

"Aw, shit, not that place." Puck huffed.

"What? What is it?"

"It's this creepy fucking building on the other side of the valley. High-rise apartments. Gives me the willies every time I go there. Weird people. Creepy building. Feral cats roaming the halls. Mean fuckers, too."

Pow.

The windows blew out like confetti in the wind, the explosion so loud that I couldn't hear right for a few minutes.

The kid held a firework, blackened and frayed around the edges. His face was soot black; his hair stood on end. He simply smiled back at us, his pearly whites taunting us with ignorance.

I'd share the conversation that ensued, but each story has a quota for the number of time you can use the word fuck, so let's not soar over that limit, and stick to the vital details. What's important is that under all the wrappers, paper bags, empty cans, and cups in the back seat, Puck owned a stash of fireworks he'd bought from right over the state line, which he kept for when a customer really pissed him off.

"Extreme cases only," he said.

I took them away from the kid, but like the flame going out, he whined and screamed. I finally gave in. Instead, I taught him to light the fireworks and toss them out the window. So, that's what he did, the whole way to the next delivery. Us, speeding along, and him, leaving a trail of smoke and percussion in our wake.

We arrived, and Puck was right. The place creeped me out, appearing darker and more obscured in the ordinary night. Inside, the florescent lights flickered with no covers. Garbage populated the front entrance as well as a few of the cats Puck mentioned.

I checked my phone. Not only was there no signal, the phone itself wouldn't turn on. I unlocked it, and it practically laughed at me, saying, "Talk to me when you're done. I've got nothing for you here."

There was no parking on the street in front of the building, so Puck parked his car in front of a hydrant again, switching on the hazards. We didn't want to leave the kid in the car, for fear he was going to set the thing on fire. So, I grabbed a handful of the fireworks and put them in my pocket to keep him occupied.

The elevator opened after a solid eight minutes. The lights were off.

"What the hell is that smell?"

"Spoiled eggs." My eyes watered.

Hesitantly, we stepped on, and when the doors closed, darkness swallowed us. Derp flicked the lighter, dimly filling the tiny room with light before letting it sink back to blackness. His skin was pale green and clammy, and the more I looked, the stringier he was. He scarcely had an ounce of muscle. Like a tree frog or a greyhound. The shadows accentuated his bony frame.

I'd never been more excited about exiting an elevator in my life, but the thrill was short lived. Cats prowled the halls as water leaked from the ceiling in several spots. Garbage cans waited outside of apartment doors with trash bags piled around them. We passed an abandoned wheelchair with a soiled diaper in the seat.

It was dark here, too. The power didn't appear to be working, as the light flickered in a strobe effect. Instead, emergency floods posted at either end of the hall created tiny pools of light. The rest of the hall was left in darkness. And for whatever reason, the Fulbright scholar that designed this fire trap used red-tinted lenses on the lights, making everything look bathed in blood.

I did my best not to touch anything as we made our way down the hall.

Derp lit a smoke bomb, and what little visibility we had became completely camouflaged.

We needed to feel our way down the hall.

I touched something wet more than once. Jerking my hand back, I wiped it on my pants, but my fingers were sticky.

I'm going to die here, aren't I?

Only half the apartments showed numbers, so we weren't sure if we had the right one when Puck knocked. It opened from the force. Inside was a murky green fog and the smell of elementary school paste.

"Hello? ChowNow. We're here with your delivery from..." Puck checked the ticket, "*Scaloppini's Chinese Bistro*?"

We both leaned in further, the floor creaking underfoot.

"Hello?" I called out.

In the back of the room, at the end of the hall, a man in a vintage gas mask and a diaper walked past.

"Oh, *hell no*." Puck dropped the food at the door and twirled to bolt. "Food's at the door. Enjoy your meal."

I grabbed Derp, and we hightailed it back.

Puck punched the button for the elevator.

And we waited.

Down at the end of the hall, the man in his leather mask bent down and picked up the food. He saw us through the fog and ambled toward us.

Puck hit the elevator button a few more times.

With the gimp getting closer, we gave up and pushed our way into the stairwell.

The lights strobed as we rushed down from floor to floor, and I nearly tripped over two different cats. One of which sliced my leg. Blood trickled.

My feet were moving too fast.

My heart thundered in my throat.

Landing after landing, the smells changed, fading into each other. Curry and hotdogs and smegma and bubblegum.

When we finally made it to the ground floor, we hurried through the lobby and back outside.

My phone came back on.

Where the station wagon once sat was now an empty space next to the hydrant.

Derp pulled on my sleeve, and I handed him a firecracker without looking.

All my attention focused on the void where the car used to be.

"Son of a bitch. Those fuckers. Took my damn car again."

"Again? You know who towed your car?"

"'Course. They get me every couple of months. Private parking lot, fire hydrant, double parked. They find anything to get me for. Honestly, I'm pretty sure they might have a tracker on my car and do it to fuck with me."

"Or, you could just park where you're supposed to." His bullshit wore on me.

"Right, and I spend thirty minutes driving around looking for a spot. Meanwhile, the food goes cold and late, and the customer takes it out on me. Trust me, Novice, it's worth it in the long run." He made his way down the street.

"Where you going?"

"They better not have touched my wallet this time. Cock gobblers always steal shit out of people's cars."

"Where are you going, Puck?" I grabbed Derp by the arm and dragged him along with us.

"To get my car. Jefferson Towing."

The name was enough to make me cringe.

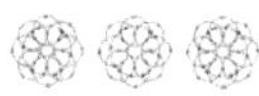

The notorious Jefferson Towing were constantly in the *Gazette* being sued or under attack from some alderman attempting to get their business license revoked. But for each tribulation they brought on themselves, they always seemed to rise to the top. Like cockroaches.

Owned by the Russian mob, a well-known front for covering up evidence or bodies, or both, everyone who worked for them was an ex-con of some sort. I'd heard horror stories dating back to when my dad was young and fresh to the city. They'd break into people's legally-parked cars and hold them for ransom, steal anything of worth from inside, and run every light on their way about the city. They had a popular song written about them by Terry Bell and the Glitter Critters called "The Independence Park Pirates."

Puck called 'em Sharks because of how predatory they were.

"Once," he told me on our long walk to the tow yard, "they towed a truck with all the proper permits and a ladder in the bed. A guy was on the ladder when they pulled away. I think he was a roofer or some shit. Anyhow, the guy falls and breaks his fucking femur. The Jefferson guys get out of their truck and make fun of the poor fuck as he's writhing on the ground. Call him all kinds of names, and in the end, drive away with his work truck. The worst is the guy who mans the window. People go to get their cars, and he calls them every kind of racial slur there is. He threatens violence—even damage to your damn car. Son of a bitch is a menace."

"How do they keep getting off? Anyone else would have gone to prison ten times over."

A cemetery on a hill to our left meant we were in Timber Ridge again, so the tow yard wasn't much further. Derp kept on behind us, lighting his firecrackers and tossing them into the air. Each time one exploded, his eyes filled, and a stupid smile crawled across his face.

"Connected. Only way to explain it. My opinion, they should burn the fucker to the ground. Then the authorities have to come onto the property. They'd get busted so quick—you *know,* they've got some shady shit back in there."

"How much does it cost to get your car out?"

We walked uphill, and though the night was cool, sweat sprouted along my back and under my arms.

Puck stopped, staring out over the graveyard.

In the cemetery stood the guy with the axe, you remember the one with the lady on the balcony in the alley? He was colossal. And though it was dark as all hell, he'd dug up a grave.

Derp lit another firecracker, and I snatched it out of his hand. His face twisted with rage, and he screeched, but I covered his mouth, tucked him under my arm, and bolted with Puck behind a stone wall. Derp struggled in my arms as I did everything I could to keep him quiet.

"What's he doing?" I asked.

"I think that's the guy. The Sundown Killer. They say he's a fucking giant." He peeked over the stone wall. "He was crouched down, and then perked his head up to look around. Don't. Move."

We were dead silent for three excruciating minutes.

"He's probably burying his victim. That's why they haven't found any bodies yet. *Wow*, that fucker is huge." Puck slunk back down behind the wall. "Follow me."

I ripped the lighter out of Derp's hand and got his attention. Crouched down we moved along the wall, Derp in tow, until he was out of sight.

"Two hundred dollars," Puck finally said.

"Huh?"

"To get the car out."

"What about what we just saw? We need to talk to the cops. If that's him, they'll finally be able to catch the guy." His change in conversation felt uncomfortable and cavalier.

"Right. Let's see how that goes. 'Excuse me, police? Yeah, we saw someone digging up a grave that fits the description of The Sundown Killer. Who is *we*? Oh, myself, a guy I'm training, and the little fuck I accidentally killed with my car but brought back to life with my delivery bag.' Come on, Novice. Right now, we need to get the car back. We can deal with what we saw later."

He had a point. If a cop showed up to take our statement, one look at Derp, and we'd be screwed. We needed to focus on the task at hand. So, we kept on, Jefferson Towing gleaming in our minds.

We stopped about a block away, where Jefferson St. and Avery St. intersected. My legs ached. I was ready for the night to be over.

Derp didn't appear to mind the cold in his running shorts, and despite his lack of clothing, he didn't have a goosebump on him. He smiled his goofy smile, oblivious to everything except the lighter's flame and the occasional *boom* of a firecracker.

"We need to figure out how we're gonna get this car out of the lot."

"Fuck, Puck. You don't have the money?"

"Like I've got that kind of scratch just laying around. *Please, Novice.* We're breaking this fucker out." He looked down the street toward the enormous neon sign with an oversized arrow pointing at the lot and seemed to contemplate our next move for a second, looking at Derp and I, then back at the sign.

"Right. Okay, so this is what we're gonna do. Novice, you and I'll slip past the chain-link fence. We'll split up and look for the wagon. Meanwhile, Derpus McTurdbrain over here'll distract the dickhead at the window. Now, I gotta warn you, they've got dogs. Mean ones. That bite. I know 'cause I tried this before on my own. Fuckers gave me ten stitches." He turned back to look at me. "Where's the kid?"

He was right there, drooling over the flame a second ago.

We searched down the street, but it was like he evaporated or something.

"Fine," Puck said. "We'll have to do it without him."

We skulked down the street.

Puck paused, pointing to a security camera hanging under the Jefferson Towing sign.

We lifted our shirts over our noses and kept to the shadows. Puck sidled up to the gate, pushed it apart and slipped through. He held the gate open for me and waved me on with a nod of the head.

"What da shit is dis?" A loud yell came from the tiny office with the thick glass window.

My whole body ceased up. I was perfectly stuck in-between the gate, fully expecting to have the dickhead at the window staring back at me. But he wasn't.

Would you believe it, Derp was exactly where he was supposed to be, preoccupying the attendant.

I took my opening and finished sliding through the gate.

Inside, cars stacked on cars in piles six high. Some were crushed, others waited their turn. A damn maze. I had no idea how we'd navigate this place, let alone get Puck's car back, but we split up nonetheless, as the guy in the office yelled at Derp.

"Hey, you. Get da fuck out my office. Where's ya fucking clothes? You're not some kinda homo or something? I don't deal with no homos."

I stayed close to the stacks to remain in the shadows, doubting we'd find Puck's car. They probably crushed it already. And if not, every car in there was a piece of shit. Puck's wagon was one turd in a mountain range of piled scat.

Then, I heard them. The dogs. Rolling, gargling growls coming from behind me.

Puck hadn't lied.

A Rottweiler and a pit bull crouched, baring their teeth. I was moments away from my jugular becoming a chewed toy. Their eyes narrowed, preparing to pounce, then *boom.*

The dogs cowered.

Boom. Boom. Boom.

They ran off, down an alley of stacked cars and out of view.

Bright flashes came from the office. Derp, that beautiful little idiot, was setting off fireworks in the glass-encased entrance.

Around the other side of a stack, an engine started.

"*Novice*. I got it. Meet me at the front."

I twirled back the way I came.

But in the corner of my eye, I spotted something that didn't register at first.

Flames.

I stopped halfway to the fence.

Inside the little office, Derp lit smoke bombs, black cats, ground spinners, roman candles, fountains, and aerial repeaters. He'd light one, slip it under the opening in the glass, and *crack bam boom*, the sucker ignited in a cloud of chaos.

A cacophony of blasts ignited.

Papers caught fire as the dickhead inside struggled to make his way to the door. The scene was beautifully terrifying—glorious even.

A car honked behind me, and I snapped back to reality.

Puck was behind the wheel, zooming by as dirt kicked up behind him. "Get in."

I ran after the station wagon and caught up near the front gate.

I hopped in the front, slamming the door. "What now? Gates still locked."

"Like I said. We're busting out."

Puck slammed his foot on the gas, and the car took off headlong into the chain-link fence.

Off to the side of us, black smoke billowed out of the windows. The asshole was trapped inside, trying to throw a desk chair through the window.

The car hit the fence at full speed but bounced back from the stretch of the chain-link. “Fuck.”

The office glass finally shattered, and the dickhead inside rolled out. His comb over stood on end. A wispy mustache rested below his fat nose. He wrestled to his feet and saw us, made to yell, but coughed instead.

The office gave way, collapsing in on itself, and with it, came down the fence.

We were free.

Puck hit the gas and off-roaded it over the chain-link and barbwire to the street.

“Hold on. We gotta get Derp,” I said.

He slammed on the brakes, and I darted out.

There he stood, in the middle of the street, eyes popping out at the flames he’d created.

I tossed him in the back seat again. As we drove away, he plastered his face to the window.

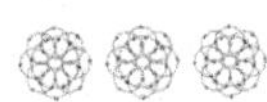

The night was over. Deliveries stopped coming in, so Puck dropped me where we’d started the night.

I took Derp with me in hopes I might find his family, but two years later, the kid is still with me. He’s kind of more like a pet than anything else. Don’t get me wrong, he’s a person. But barely. Most nights, he sits shotgun with me, in my turd on wheels, and we deliver food around the valley. He doesn’t eat, which is weird. Doesn’t sleep either. Though with each day that passes, he seems to get a little better, a little smarter, a tad bit more normal.

As for Puck, I saw him around, passing each other on our way to a delivery. Give a quick beep beep—a shout out on the dispatch chat line. But it wasn’t long after that night he moved on. Heard he quit. Something about not being on good terms with the guy who started ChowNow and not wanting to work for minimum wage at a company he’d started.

Oh, and we made an anonymous call to the police about the guy in the cemetery. They still haven’t caught the giant. They have, on the other hand, caught a few photos of him and put them up all over town. It was him all right.

The police do say they're "very close" to catching him. Not sure what they plan to do once they track him down. Bastard is as big as a mountain and twice as wide.

I pray I don't run into him while I'm out one night.

Anyhow, that's my story. The craziest night I ever had on the job.

Not sure what they told you in your interview, but shit has a tendency to get weird out here. My best advice to you, Novice, is to drive fast, watch out for tow trucks, get those cash tips when you can, and for the love of Christ, don't hit anyone.

Best of luck to you.

Now, get out there and make some money.

VIII.

There are few places Jinx dared not go, like Haymarket General Hospital. He used to say, "I'd rather have dinner at de house of de Devil himself den spen even a minute an a half at de ole Hayma'ket." Perhaps, he knew the government services would hassle him for living on life's periphery for so long. Or maybe it was due to the many lives both gained and lost under one roof. Possibly, it was because he still remembered the last time he was checked into the mental health ward. He'd been forced to escape and at a great cost. Whatever the reason, never was a man more terrified of the words Haymarket General Hospital. Upon seeing the massive institution, he'd spin on his heels and go until it was out of sight.

On the night Jinx mounted his escape, he'd hidden in the children's wing, under the bed of little Millie Anderson. Jinx was practically long-gone when a sheepdog attacked him in the dark. He thrashed and fought free but left behind a sizeable chunk of his being.

Millie died the next day.

And Jinx forever asked himself why a sheepdog was in a hospital to begin with.

HAYMARKET MAGGIE

In Lakeview, people tell the legend of a dog. Many argue the lore is nothing more than a children's story. I know different. In the 1920's, a little girl, Millie Anderson, owned a shaggy sheepdog named Maggie. The dog grew fond of the girl and took care of her, as any nanny or mother might. She helped teach the girl to walk, to swim, and even joined her at mid-afternoon tea.

When Mary turned seven, she was diagnosed with polio. They ushered her away and quarantined her in a far-corner ward of the Haymarket General Hospital, built on the site of Lakeview's former Haymarket neighborhood. Alone and afraid, Millie cried all night.

But, after a week, she stunned the doctors when she stopped crying, for Maggie the sheepdog rested across the little girl's legs. Security came to remove the dog, but it growled, baring its white teeth, not allowing anyone near Millie unless she gave them permission. There the dog stayed, across her feet, for eight months, until one fateful winter's night the girl passed in her sleep.

For two days, Maggie allowed no one near Millie's body. At night, the dog's whimpers trailed through the halls as she licked the girl's face.

Millie was buried in the graveyard on the hillside of a small hamlet known as Timber Ridge. There, Maggie made her way through the city, following the scent of her young master.

The day after they buried the girl, the caretaker woke for his morning rounds to find Maggie sleeping atop the tiny grave. He did all he could to coax the dog out of the cemetery, bribing it with bones and balls and even a T-bone steak. Nothing worked. Maggie stayed put, undeterred and loyal to her girl.

For six years, Maggie slept on top of Millie's grave, sometimes so stationary passersby mistook her for a statue, until they heard the whimpers coming from the scraggly pile of hair. Maggie stayed in spite of snow and rain and gale force winds. She remained upon the grave until she died, at the age of fifteen, continuing to wait for her little girl to return to her. Her remains were buried next to Millie's grave with a small headstone.

That's not the part people want to contest, though some details may have been added for dramatic effect. No, the part people dispute is this: A year after the dog's passing, it was spotted at the hospital, howling up at the room the girl once occupied. When orderlies engaged the dog, it disappeared. People chalked it up to a coincidence, arguing it was a different dog altogether.

But sure enough, that following year, the dog visited the hospital again. This time, the security guard on duty followed it for three blocks until he lost it in the shadows. Each year, on the anniversary of the dog's death, Maggie reappears, a gaggle of ghost story enthusiasts in tow. They say you can, sometimes, see her clear as day, and other times, you can hardly hear her whimper. But always, she leads the people in the direction of the graveyard, where devotees believe she goes to rest up for the coming year.

The story, whether true or not, has attracted quite a bit of attention over the years. In 1974, a plaque was erected outside the door of the room little Millie Anderson once stayed in. That's how I came upon the tale.

In truth, the idea of a ghost dog seemed as absurd as the legends of Ya'hootie, the terrible sasquatch that roamed the hills, but we all know how that turned out. Yet, in my reluctance to believe such a far-fetched tale of love and devotion, I set out one year with a group of true believers. By night's end, I would devoutly join their fray. I not only witnessed the bushy dog with my own eyes, but I felt it as it passed by my leg. Upon its touch, a shiver grew inside of me, crawling up my back as if my spine froze from the inside out.

For years, I followed Maggie and her cries through the streets of Lakeview, always losing her along the way. One year, I decided to change my approach. While everyone was so focused on following her path from the beginning, I decided to go to the supposed destination: the little girl's grave.

All night, I waited as the cold wind blew hard, freezing my bones. I found a spot across from Millie's grave and leaned myself up against a tombstone. Soon, the darkness faded, giving way to the light of the sun right beyond the valley ridge.

Exhausted and on the verge of sleep, I heard a jingling chime. A sheepdog sat in front of me, licking my face, and its cold, wet tongue shuddered me awake. She barked once, a happy bark, as if to say *thank you.*

But for what? I did not know.

I leaned closer, and around its singing collar read the name: Maggie.

As if a giant boot of joy and fear and absolute sadness kicked me in the chest, I felt the sudden need to cry.

Those black eyes fed me all the desperation and loneliness Maggie endured for so many years. And with that, she passed her burden on to me. The dog walked over to the girl's grave, laid down, and at first light, she disappeared into the ground.

As I stood up to leave, I swear I heard, somewhere in the distance, the laughter of a little girl. I've been back since, bringing with me witnesses to see the amazing truth of the dog that never left.

Yet, in all my visits since, I've never heard more than a faint tinkle on the wind.

IX.

Jinx never could trust his eyes. He had a long and storied history of never knowing if the things he saw were real or a product of his imagination. It was for this reason, one day while riding the SkyTram, that he assumed he was just seeing things. The tram had been empty save one man sitting, as usual, at the other end of the car. He was thin, slightly balding, and a clean-shaven face. The man wore glasses with thin frames, a sweater and collared shirt underneath. Jinx paid him only as much attention as to know he was there. The vagrant pinned his head against the window and closed his eyes for his third nap of the day.

But before the next stop, he heard a deep guttural growl. When he opened his eyes, the man on the train was entirely different. His face, his hair, his size—everything about him screamed that this was a different man. But the train had not stopped, and no gush of wind that came from a passenger changing cars. The only things still remaining were the clothes and the thin glasses. The bum squinted his eyes, confused by the conundrum, but after a moment, he rested his head.

THE LION'S DEN

The reason so many interpretations of love exist is because we all experience it differently. No two people are alike. That's a given. The affection you know with one person will always be different than the worship you have with another. In fact, the person you are in love with may experience love completely different than the way *you* understand it towards *them*. No matter how similar the feeling may be. That doesn't mean you'll experience it the way you did the first time. You can never go back home, they say. And, you can never step into the same river twice. They say that one all the time. I say, love is *always* different.

This all inevitably comes down to two major factors: time and life. Time because it only moves in one direction, and life because it's unavoidable.

Countless poets and musicians have strained to define love in masterful works of art.

Everyone, down to a stranger at the bus stop has an opinion on the matter.

And they are all different.

No matter how many ways we yearn to express it, the feeling can't be defined. Perhaps that's what makes love so interesting.

Regardless, it exists.

Love is real.

That is why when I tell you I love two women, you know I mean it. Equally. Without bias. I love them and will never be able to decide between them. For, as different as the women I care for are from each other, so am I from myself…

Where am I?

I have that old scrambled feeling in my brain again. Like my gray matter is being served up for breakfast.

I'm coughing. I've been coughing for some time. I strain to catch my breath. An empty cough syrup bottle lies on the floor with the cap off. I slow my breathing and concentrate on what is in front of me.

A steering wheel. Fuzzy dice swing on the rearview mirror. I'm in my car.

The windshield wipers slosh patiently, clearing the buildup of scattered droplets upon the glass.

I'm parked.

The car is on, so I shut it off. The wipers stop mid stroke.

Out the window, identical row houses line a gloomy street.

Where am I?

This is not where I live. I've never seen this road in my damn life. But I know, before my eyes focus on the street signs, I'm at Willow and Burden. Not quite The Bog, but not far either. Humbert Square.

How did I know that? What the hell is going on?

I get out of the car, and the familiar stench of backed up sewers permeates the neighborhood, carried on each drop. The rain is soft but consistent, like a routine.

What brought me here?

A tiny yellow house with a sliver of lawn and a chain link fence glows to my right. Half-dead bushes and flowers wheeze their death rattle at me. But something inside me says to go closer. I can't help it, my feet move, dictating where I go.

The least I can do is lock the car, so I reach into my pocket and press the fob.

Bee-doop.

I freeze at the door.

What am I doing? None of this makes any sense.

I want to go home, snuggle up with Iris, and watch TV. But the same something that told me to approach the house is also telling me to open the door. It's locked. Thank God. That might have been creepy.

On a whim, maybe out of muscle memory, I use the keys in my hand and flip through until I see one I don't recognize. I try it, and the door opens. This is too weird to stop now.

I walk inside and find two more doors. The one on the right is open with stairs going up, so I follow them. Each step creaks with a familiar groan that I anticipate before it happens.

At the top, I use my key again and let myself into a converted attic/studio apartment. It's dark and musty with wood floors. The ceiling slants to a point, making me claustrophobic.

Against one wall is a bed, the bed I used when I was a child. I thought I trashed it a few years ago when Iris and I needed a new one. The sheets are unmade and smell of use. Across from the bed is a dresser with a TV on top. Both are mine. Both, like the bed, I threw away years ago. A pile of folded clothes is on the dresser, and a closer look reveals that they are my old baby clothes. What are they doing here?

On a side table, next to the bed, I find a framed picture of a woman I don't know. She is beautiful and blowing the camera a kiss. She has short dark hair, a nose ring, and the two happiest eyes I've ever seen. Next to the frame is a wristwatch with a leather band. I've been looking for it since I was a boy. Thought I'd lost it.

What is going on?

As depressing as the apartment might appear, it has an air of joy to it. Like the people who live here love each other so much, it's been absorbed by the walls.

The door opens behind me, and in walks the woman in the photo. She's sporting a worn, black hoodie and a ribbed white undershirt. She is carrying two handfuls of plastic bags. Her stunning face is beautiful in a calming and unassuming way. When she smiles at me, an alarm inside me flares, an explosion of euphoria. She wears baggy clothes, but I distinctly see a tiny bulge in her belly. She's not fat; her frame is too slender. She must be pregnant. There's a tickle in my throat again, and I cough.

"Hey, Cash, help me with these groceries, would you?"

Who the hell is Cash?

When I wake up, I'm in bed next to my wife. The room is dark, pervaded by the blue-gray of night.

Just a dream.

Fucking weird.

Maybe Iris is right, I *should* lay off the red meat.

I take a deep breath to calm myself.

It was so damn real. I've never dreamt like that before. Nothing a little spooning won't cure. So, I roll over and throw my arm over Iris, first stroking hers, then her breast. She's sleeping in the nude again. I love when she does. Makes me feel like more of a man. I cup her breast, and it takes me a second before I realize they've gotten smaller. Significantly. She's lost a lot of weight recently but not like this. This isn't even the same shape.

She shrugs in her sleep, and I move my hand to her waist where I pull at her hip. But, instead of her soft stomach, I find a stiff bulging belly.

The woman who is not Iris rolls over to see me with her smiling face and sleepy eyes. "Hi."

I pull away abruptly and fall out of bed with a yelp. The table light clicks on from the other side of the bed. "Cash? Cash, baby, what's the matter?"

I scramble to my feet and, in the faint light, discover I'm as nude as she is. I don't sleep naked. *Too* emancipating. I've been a boxers and a tee-shirt man ever since I was ten.

Not cool.

Who took my clothes?

I grab a pillow to cover up and find myself in the apartment from my dream.

No. Not a dream.

"Cash, what's going on? You're scaring me." Her face is tired, but pursed, showing distinct concern.

"Who the fuck is *Cash*?"

"You are—oh, Jesus." Her eyes go wide as I clearly come into focus.

"Oh Jesus, what? Who are you? Where is my wife? Why the *fuck* am I naked?"

"Oh, God." She looks up at the ceiling, straining to think. "Rob?"

"Okay, that's better-ish. Why do you know my name?"

The table lamp illuminates her nude form, holding her breasts.

She covers up, like I'd walked in on her changing, going pale and shy. "I, ah, um. I'm Ingrid. Your, I mean, Cash's…"

I know it before she says it. "Wife?"

"Kinda, yeah."

"Who is Cash?" What kind of a stupid name is Cash, anyway? It reminds me of the kind of name a pimp gives his illegitimate son.

"Maybe you should just go. You shouldn't be here." Her tummy pushes out the sheet wrapped around it, highlighting her protruding belly button.

"Fine by me. Where are my clothes?" I search the room, but it's dark.

"Over there, on the chair." She points into the shadows, but I know exactly where to go. I put on my clothes quick and head for the door. I haven't finished buttoning my shirt before I'm at the top of the stairs.

I turn back to her.

"Who is Cash?"

The words coming out of her mouth are fuzzy and faded, but they hit me as if stepping in front of a bus.

"You are."

Everything goes black.

What fucking day is it?

Like that matters, Rob.

When was the last time you knew what month it was?

My throat itches as I clear it again. My brain is mush.

What is happening to me?

I need answers. This shit is getting old.

I'm standing at the Lakeview Botanical Gardens, a large complex of glass bubbles, housing all varieties of flora, on the edge of the city. Inside it is lush and green. But, I'm outside, and it's snowing. When did it become snowing weather? It was cool and raining just yesterday.

That *was* yesterday, wasn't it?

Christ, Rob, get a grip.

I trudge up the shoveled path, along the walk, to the entrance. This is where Iris works. I've always thought it was funny a woman named for a flower works in a garden, but she's always been good with that stuff. She says she takes after her mother.

I see her through the glass doors, inside at the help desk. She perks up when she sees me, and I wave at her to come outside. Her smile feels so much better, like coming home. I sense that I haven't seen it in weeks—months even. Iris meets me outside, on a bench I brush the snow off of, and gives me a kiss.

"Hey, babe. What you doing here? I thought you were supposed to be with Dr. Guise today." She sounds sincerely surprised and excited to see me. She leans over, and I plant another kiss on her like I haven't seen her in years. Maybe I haven't. At this point, who knows?

"I…don't know."

I don't remember how I got here. My car isn't parked nearby.

I shift to face her head on. "I think there's something I need to tell you about. Last night—or I think it was last night—I don't know anymore. I found myself in this weird apartment, with this woman… I thought it was a dream at first, but it was too real. What was her name? Ingrid. I don't know how I got there, but…"

How in the world does someone approach this conversation rationally? It's not like I expect her to believe me. I'm fully expecting her to flip out. But, I need to get this off my chest.

Her eyes don't appear phased at all. Maybe, she'll be able to help me make sense of it.

"She kept calling me… What was it? Cash. Does that name mean anything to you?"

Her smile drops instantly, and she twists away. "They told us this wasn't ever gonna happen. You're not supposed to know about this. Why does this keep happening?"

Now, she's panicked.

Which scares me.

She knows all right. My wife knows something and isn't telling me about it.

"Iris, what is going on? Yesterday, I wake up in front of a house I've never seen, and somehow, I have the key in my pocket. Last night, I wake up next to a pregnant woman. She seemed to know who I was at first, then treated me as a stranger. Now, I'm with you, and I can't remember how I got here. I'm really starting to freak out. I need answers."

Her face flushes, matching the color of her lips, and as mad as I am, I can't help but ache for her.

"I know," she finally says. "I know about it all."

There's that damn truck again, hitting me like a crash-test dummy. "What do you mean, you know? *What* do you know?"

"Ingrid should have called me. Any deviation, any hiccup, we're supposed to let each other and Dr. Guise know immediately."

"Hiccup?"

"Rob, honey, listen. I don't know if I'm supposed to talk to you about this. Maybe you should go see Dr. Guise. Or your mother. Maybe, she should tell you. She told me, after all."

"My mother? What are you talking about? How do you know Ingrid? Jesus. I simply want some fucking answers." Head in hands, I struggle to center my thoughts.

Note to self: pick up more cough syrup at earliest convenience. This coughing is really starting to make it hard to concentrate.

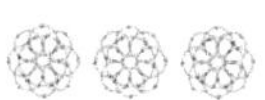

When I lift my head from my hands, I'm in an office.

It's nice with a wall of books to my right, a nice swirling mahogany desk in front of me and framed degrees filling out the other wall to my left. A man in a white lab coat sits behind the desk. Dr. Guise, I assume. He is old with a bald, liver-spotted head, and a crest of hair sticking up in back. He wears glasses and a goatee—the mustache and chin beard aren't connected.

Why is he looking at me like that? Like I'm a piece of meat on the grill; wondering if it's time to flip me yet.

Beyond him is a wall of glass overlooking the whole of the city. I know this view. I'm in BigCorp tower. The statue of Lady Columbia stares at me from outside the window.

Whatever sick carnival ride I'm on—I want off.

"Hello, Robert." His voice is a rusted saxophone, smooth and pleasing, but certainly weathered. "How are you feeling?"

"My brain burns like it's been chewing on pepper seeds. My throat is sore. Every time I cough, it quakes throughout my entire body. I'm not really sure who the fuck you are, which is making me the embodiment of anxiety. But other than that, I'm *swell*." This is me testing him. Seeing what I learn about him by getting him agitated. You learn a lot about someone in the face of anger. Fight or flight and all. I wonder what that says about me?

He smiles and grunts a laugh. "As I figured. Iris tells me you've met Ingrid. Describe to me how that felt."

"I'm sorry. Dr. Guise, right?"

He nodded.

"Maybe you could stop asking *me* questions and start answering *mine*. Like why the fuck am I here? Or, why do I keep blacking out? Why is my wife hiding things from me? Or even, the overarching—what in the holy fuck is going on?"

"My apologies, Robert. I am Dr. Adolfus Guise. I must say, this is all very exciting. We've been waiting to see how this might turn out. Do forgive me. I've been known to forget my bedside manner." He leans forward and clasps his hands, like a child about to open a present. "Robert, this is going to be difficult for you to accept, but I need you to stay with me."

He says the last bit as though I'm gonna up and leave, which since I'm considering it, doesn't sound like a bad idea.

"You have what we like to call dissociative identity disorder, or DID, also known as multiple personalities. It's extremely rare. It merely exists in one-to-three percent of the general population and is three-to-nine times more likely in females than males, which is one of the many factors making your case so noteworthy. Though the exact cause is widely debated, many in my field argue it originates through trauma at a young age. Much like PTSD." He pauses to clean his lenses. "However, your case, Robert, is quite unique. You see, while you undoubtedly experienced trauma at a young age, *you* have a physical transformation as well. A metamorphosis of sorts, fully transfiguring you from one alter to the next."

My head is swimming. This guy is nuts, right? This happens in bad movies and Victorian horror novels. Not to me. Not in real life. Walking out on this guy keeps sounding better and better. But part of me won't stand up. Part of me can't help but ask, "Alter?"

"I'm sorry. An alter is the term we use for your alternate personalities. Up until now, we've merely observed one, going by the name Cash. Or Cashmere, your middle name." When he says it out loud, it makes me wince. I've always hated that name. It's a family name, sure, but it doesn't mean it's worth passing on.

"Up until now?"

"Yes, well…you see, Cash has been a part of your life since you were young. He is virtually your opposite in every way imaginable. Even physically, though you resemble one another, he is characteristically different. While you go clean shaven, he has a thick five o'clock shadow. His hairline is different. He's thinner, taller, and more muscular."

"So me…if I were a male model."

He replaced his glasses, humor lining his face. "Yes, you might put it that way. Cash is everything you've ever wanted to be but fell short on. Though, I don't want you to assume I'm saying he is in any way the more-perfect you. Cash definitely has his flaws. He's crass. He's manipulative. He lights up the room with charisma but doesn't know when to shut it off. A chronic philanderer and chauvinist. Frankly, if I might speak from personal taste, he gives me the willies."

Well it's not all bad. At least, I'm not completely the crummiest version of me. Things could be worse. "You were saying, 'Up until now.'"

"Up until now, Cash has been your lone alter. At least, with what we've observed. For years, it has simply been the two of you. Not once were you aware of the presence of the other. As you grew, you followed different paths. You dated different women. Kept different groups of friends. Worked different jobs. You majored in Earth Science, while he majored in Communications. You even married different women. I must say, between the two, you have always been the more intelligent. The two of you have gone on for many years simply living your separate lives. If ever an instance came up where Cash might be revealed to you, or vice versa, you immediately blanked. A temporary loss of hearing or blindness. Sometimes, you'd look directly at something, and your brain refused to register what it was." His glasses reflect the window, creating an endless mirror. "But recently, there has been some…slippage. Your alternate lives have begun to overlap on one another. Cash as it seems is…for a lack of a better word, dying."

Say what?

"I'm dying?"

"No, no, no. You—Robert—are healthy as you've ever been. It's Cash who is dying off. We believe this is due to one of two possibilities. Either you are beginning to come to terms with the trauma you experienced as a child and no longer need the alter…or he is being killed off in order to make room for another alter we have yet to observe in full stasis."

"How long?" Suddenly, I'm panicked over the death of some guy I've never even met. None of me wants to believe he's telling the truth.

"There's no saying, really. Cash might be gone as we speak, or he could malinger along for years."

"No. I mean, when did this start?" Iris knows. She knew all about this. Why didn't she tell me? *Like you'd believe her, Rob.* This doctor's telling you, and you hardly believe him.

"Oh. Well, you began exhibiting symptoms around nine, right after your trauma. At first, your mother says she assumed you were playing, like any normal child. But soon, for brief periods of time, you started answering only to the name Cash. That's when she brought you to me."

I can't take my gaze off the glare of his shiny bald head. There's certain things a person tends to remember. That would be one of them, right? And yet, this man still registers as a stranger in my brain.

"Why don't I remember you? If I've been coming to see you since I was nine, why don't I remember you?"

Answer that one, asshole. Gonna tell me I've got a split personality. Too many holes.

"Hypnosis." When he says it, it's like someone reassuring me there's leprechauns protecting pots of gold at the end of rainbows. "It's a common treatment in these cases. To ease you through the treatment, I hypnotized you to believe you were watching television or a movie."

That's convenient.

"If I'd treated you outright at such a young age, it might have been catastrophic to your mental health. You might have gone catatonic. It's imperative to ease a subject through their treatment as peacefully as possible."

"Hypnosis? You know how hokey you sound, right? So, I'm guessing you've taken me out of hypnosis because of this, slippage, as you put it?"

Watching TV? Now I understand why nobody ever knew what show I'd been talking about all these years. And, why I kept watching, despite the fact I never really found it interesting to begin with.

"You always were the more perceptive one." He takes off his glasses and cleans them again. Breathing on the lenses—*hah*—then wiping them clean.

Seriously, how dirty can one man's glasses be?

"When your mother brought you to me, we worked for years with no success. When you were about thirteen, I administered you a new medication created by the scientists here at BigCorp. XR-21. It was experimental and kept off the books, but I assured your mother this might be our last hope. She gave me permission to use you in our case study. The results were, to say the least, astounding. The XR-21 triggered a natural growth hormone in your cells, which became the harbinger for your transformation. Though, we hadn't expected it, you changed physically, for the first time, fully becoming the living embodiment of your alter. I told you, in hypnosis, the XR-21 was simply cough syrup."

How does he know about the cough syrup? This isn't at all funny anymore.

A scam. He's running some sort of elaborate con on me or something.

"So, you're telling me I'm taking an experimental drug, which alters me into a completely different person? And this is legal, how?"

"No. Not at all. The XR-21 is administered to limit your switching back and forth. When you were a child you advanced to the point where you switched so frequently, every other word might be given by a different alter. Your mother was worried beyond belief. With each switch, your health deteriorated. You grew sicker and sicker."

That's why I missed all of the eighth grade. But *they* told me it was mono. Fuck, I don't know what to believe.

He slips his glasses back on and a flare of light skips off his head and past my eyes. "For all intents and purposes, the XR-21 saved your life. The transformation was a side effect. The drug simply limited your switching. But, when you did switch, it was a full transfiguration."

My clothes are tight.

It's not hot in here, but I'm definitely sweating.

"Sorry, I just…I don't believe it. Any of this. It's impossible. Science and nature don't work like that. You're gonna have to prove it to me. I appreciate this wild story. Truly, well executed. You nearly had me. But until I see some proof…it's all bullshit." There we go. Stick with the facts. You can't fake hard data.

"I anticipated you'd say something along those lines. Always the scientist, Robert. It's probably what I appreciate about you most." He pivots to the wall of books. A television framed in the center flips on. "These are some of our earliest case studies with you. If for any reason it gets to be too much, please let me know."

"It's a little late for that, doc."

On the screen, I'm sitting on a table in a doctor's office. I'm about thirteen—skinny and gawky, desperately emaciated—sitting on the examination table in my boxers. I'm comatose, staring into nothing.

I don't remember any of this. A voice off screen speaks. "Subject has extreme deterioration of immune system due to MPD switching. We are administering XR-21 for the first time. Subject will stay in isolation as we observe the effects of the drug and record our data. Please note the subject has been placed in a catatonic state via hypnosis to ease his way through the process."

A man walks on screen in a lab coat, a younger version of Dr. Guise with a full crop of curly hair. "Cash, can you hear me?"

"Yes." My voice is detached.

"You have quite a nasty cough. I'm going to give you some cough syrup to make it all better. Is that all right?"

"Is it cherry? I only like cherry."

I hate cherry. I hate all cough syrup. It's been a struggle for me my whole life.

Guise faces the camera and smiles. "Yes. It is the best-tasting cherry medicine you've ever had. Now, open up." I open my mouth, and he pours me a dose. "Mmm. Now, wasn't that tasty?"

"Yes."

I shiver a little in my seat, imagining the taste of cough syrup in my mouth.

Guise stares at the monitors recording data, then it switches, and his voice continues over some rudimentary graphics. "Over the past week, the subject has responded successfully to the XR-21. Subject's health has improved while the switching between personalities has decreased significantly. Blood pressure is down, white blood cell count is up, and muscle mass is beginning to regenerate. We will continue to administer XR-21. As of yet, the subject has reduced switching from ten to fifteen times per hour to merely twice a day.

"However, there have been some astonishing side effects none of us foresaw. While the subject's switching has greatly decreased, when he does take on his alter-personality, a full metamorphosis is achieved. The subject changes physically, now, in addition to his mental state." A shot of a boy on the same examination table comes on screen. His hair is different. Darker and shorter. His face is different. Leaner and more angular. His build is broader and filled out. This is not *me* as a boy. I've never seen this kid before.

"Subject has grown two inches in height. Hair color has darkened. Facial features are radically different. And he has begun to use his left hand predominantly over his right. After the transformation, subject answers solely to the name of Cashmere, or Cash, the original subject's middle name. Any mention of the name Robert is blocked out, much like before. As though the initial subject has been erased completely. We caught the transformation live, on film, after hours of relentless monitoring."

Loud, hacking yawps shake the boy on screen's whole body. His hair lightens with every shudder, as if he's shaking the color from each lock.

What the hell—he's shrinking.

It looks like he's inside an invisible trash compactor. His face twitches. The nose abruptly shifts and grows. The brow line sinks in.

Jesus, what is this guy making me watch? This is disgusting. I might puke.

It's like all the bones in his face shatter under an invisible pressure. Shortly, the boy stops shaking and is unnaturally still. He looks up at the camera.

Bullshit. It's not possible. That's…me.

I'm healthier looking. I don't look so pale. But strike me down if that's not me.

I face Guise at his desk. "You've got to be fucking kidding me with this shit. I see it. I know it happened. But it's just…not computing."

"We reacted much the same at first. For a long time, I fought the notion. It was simply too much for me to process. It took your mother quite a while to get over as well."

I imagine my mother in hysterics at watching me change into this other person. When I was a boy, she was really distant for a period. I assumed it was because I was getting older, going through puberty. Nothing like this.

"Eventually, like us all, she came around. Surprisingly well, to be honest. She took on this new boy as though he were a completely different son. She loved him, cared for him, and made sure your and his lives never intersected. Without your mother, Robert, I can't say you and Cash would have ever made it this far."

I spring out of my chair and pace the room in no discernible direction.

I want to process this. What's getting me, surprisingly, isn't so much the fact that I transform into a completely different guy half the time.

Though, it's still fucking weird.

Everyone around me knows and hasn't told me.

Everyone knows more about me than I do.

I'm violated, like I've been molested in a mob of people, and when I look to see who did it, it was everyone.

"There's more," he says. "I have one more interview to show you. If you'd please take a seat."

He motions toward the leather armchair, and I sit down.

The screen shows this room. The camera is pointed directly at my chair. A man with dark buzzed hair is sitting where I am now. He's wearing a white and blue button up with a gingham pattern—Wait. I look down at my shirt. Fucking white and blue button up with a gingham pattern.

I see where this is going.

Though the man is bigger than me, more solid, more handsome, he looks sick. He wears shadows under his eyes. His nose is red and irritated. And his skin, though darker than mine, has a clammy-green hue.

Guise is off screen. "Cash, how are we feeling today?"

"Like a shit sundae on the hottest day of the year. I'm sick, you fuck nut, what'd you think?" His voice doesn't sound like me in the slightest. It's harsher, like he smokes a pack a day and drinks a fifth for lunch. It's truck tires on gravel.

"Anything new at home?"

"Just found out Ingrid's gonna have a boy. Pretty stoked about that."

Stoked? Who the hell says stoked?

"To be honest, she's the only thing that makes being sick bearable." His face brightens when he talks about Ingrid. And down deep, I have an anxious infatuation-flutter at the mention of her name. Like I can't imagine ever being without the stranger I encountered only the other night.

"Are you continuing to philander behind her back?"

"How did you—Yeah." He's quiet for a second. "I can't help myself. I love Ingrid, doc, I do. But it's like I see a woman making eyes at me, and *bam*, before I know what happened, I'm in bed with her. It's like I'm fucking bloodthirsty or something. I might be in a bar, an elevator, in line at Jackalope Jerry's. Doesn't matter. Suddenly, I'm in the stairwell, or the bathroom, or some stranger's apartment, pumping away, pants around my ankles. Licking every inch, nibbling on nipples… Afterwards, I realize what I've done, and I'm ashamed. Fuck. I hate myself. But sure enough, the next set of eyes lands on me, and there I am again. Off to the races. Don't get me wrong. I was doing it in the moment. Because, when you're already balls de—I mean, sorry, inside of a chick, there's no backing out then. But whatever it was that brought me to that point. That ain't me."

He slumps over as he's talking. What a fuckhead this guy is. I don't know Ingrid, but I know what it was like after my bachelor party with Iris. I felt the same way. Like I was doing things I couldn't control.

"Cash, as you know, unfortunately you don't have much time."

"Just say it, doc. I'm fucking dying."

"Have you made any plans with Ingrid for when you are gone?"

He wipes away the tears running down his face. "No. I mean, there's my mom. I'm sure she'll help. It's her grandkid after all. But financially? No. We hardly scrape enough to pay rent each month, let alone savings."

"What if I told you there was a person who'd be able to help Ingrid? Someone you've never met. But you needed to convince him. What would you say?"

He looks up at Guise behind the camera. "For real?"

"Suppose it was. What might you say?"

He pleads to the camera directly.

"I'd say, I love Ingrid more than life itself. I'm scared shitless of the idea she's gonna be a mother all on her own. She's the best damn thing that's ever happened to me. I'm letting her down. I'm about to become the ultimate deadbeat dad. All I ever wanted was for her to be happy. The first time I laid eyes on Ingrid, she was taking my order at a restaurant, and I went straight puppy dog for her. I fuck a lot of women. I'm a scumbag. I won't deny it. But Ingrid and my baby deserve better. They deserve more than what I've given them. If you're willing to help…I need your help. I'm desperate." He peers back at Guise. "How's that?"

The video pauses. The truth of every word sits in my spine. The way he feels about Ingrid is the same way I did when I first saw her. I haven't felt anything like it since Iris and I met. Knowing that he screws around on Ingrid makes me want to take a baseball bat to his face. But I want to empathize with him, too.

"As I'm sure you've guessed, this was taken a few moments before you and I started this conversation. I've treated the two of you for over twenty years now, Robert. In that time, as unprofessional as it might be, I've grown attached to you both. It pains me to see Cash like this. He's not a bad person, simply flawed. And it's been a great stress on my brain knowing Ingrid might be left to fend for herself. She's known all along of the possibilities, as I've held some one-on-one sessions with her. And I tell you, she is deeply troubled about all this."

My heart aches for this interloper, this foreigner, in my life.

"I'm asking you to please consider bringing her into your family. Obviously, you'll need to discuss it with Iris. But please know when Cash does go, she was never legally married to him the way you and Iris are. Cash has no social security number or birth certificate. She has no rights to anything. But before you can help, you need to come to terms with your childhood trauma. If you don't, another alter might soon move in and take the place of Cash. Or worse—yourself."

It's a lot to process.

"You keep mentioning this trauma in my childhood, but I don't what you're talking about." To be honest, I don't really remember my childhood. Nothing before age nine or ten, at least.

He peers out the window again. It's as if, for the first time, he's afraid to speak. "Some things, Robert, are better for me to tell you. The medical, psychological, scientific information, for example. Other questions your mother should answer. I hate to string you along, but the trauma is one of them."

Answer one question, you get fifty more. This is no way to live.

Finding my car was an undertaking. I don't remember where I parked, or having driven, so it takes me an hour of walking around downtown. I stuck with it though, because Guise assured me I drove.

The snow from before, with Iris, is gone.

How long has it been? I can't keep track.

The whole drive out to my mom's place in the suburbs, I'm understandably distracted. But the monotony of it eases my brain and gives me a little relief.

Something familiar.

Something that hasn't drastically changed.

Traffic is the same. Exits are the same. The trees swallowing you up are the same. Same curves. Same lights. Driving through the Arbor Sanctuary is about as much a relief as I've known in what I imagine is months.

Please don't tell me it's been months.

The driveway is empty. My mom still lives in my childhood home. After the drive between here and BigCorp tower, I appreciate all the times she must have driven me back and forth. Some parents drive their kids all over for a traveling soccer team or violin lessons. My mom drove me because I had another person living inside of me.

How did the college admissions board deal with that little ditty?

The front door is bright pink. That's my mom for you. She knows who she is and what she likes, despite how different it is. Wish I could say the same.

She never locks the door, so I walk right in.

"Mom? You home?"

"Hey, honey, in here," she calls from the kitchen. Chocolate chip cookies rest on the air. She makes them when stressed. Makes sense why I put on so much weight when I was a kid. The more I consider my youth, the more it appears to tell a hidden story.

Thank God, I'm the smarter one…

Row upon row of cookies are cooling on racks. Three plates are already piled high around the room. When she sees me, she comes over and gives me a kiss. Her hair is greasy and frazzled, like she hasn't showered in days. The bags under her eyes tell the same story.

I gesture to the dessert disks encroaching on the kitchen. "I think you've got enough."

"Oh, I, ah, needed to bake. You know how I get." Her eyes betray her. There's worry there. True, visceral fear.

"*Right.* Mom, put the spatula down," I say as jokingly and lighthearted as I can.

She forces a smile.

"We need to talk."

Her smile disappears.

"'Kay. S'pose you're right."

I follow her into the living room, and we take a seat on either side of the coffee table. She won't look at me, swiping the streak of gray running down the center of her hair; does its existence have anything to do with me?

My mother has always kept a tidy house, and being an empty nester, she's finally able to have the designer and antique furniture she's always wanted. The couch is stiff and uncomfortable with a floral pattern. Furniture should make you struggle with the idea of ever getting up, but this damn thing is like a torture device from the Inquisition.

"I met with Dr. Guise."

"I know. He called."

"He showed me the videos of me…and Cash."

"Yeah." She can't look in my direction for more than a few seconds, like making eye contact with me is a painful endeavor.

"Mom, enough. I need you to look at me. Why keep this from me? Guise kept talking about some fucking trauma. What trauma?"

I get her full attention, but she strains to find the words.

"I didn't know what to do, Rob. You were so young and constantly getting sicker. Dr. Guise assured me, if we told you about Cash, it might be harmful to your overall health. He always said there'd be a right time to let you know, but after you started with the changing, the prospect of telling you kept getting pushed further and further back. It was hard enough caring for one son as a single parent. Then, overnight, *two*. Two sons with different clothing sizes. Two sons with two appetites and two groups of friends and two sets of interests and two entirely different styles of rebellion. You have to understand, honey, I was overwhelmed."

"So, you kept the charade up into my adulthood? Mom—I'm married—to two different women. One of which is pregnant." I'm so mad. I'm having trouble collecting my thoughts. My mother has a way of doing that to me.

Secrets suck. I'm so fucking exposed.

"Honey, you're having a hard-enough time coming to terms with this now. Imagine how difficult this might have been as a *child*."

She has a point. "How many people know? Answer me that."

"Everyone." She says it as a fact.

"What do you mean everyone?"

"I mean, every time you met new friends, got a job, dated girls—I was right there to explain the situation. Lots of people were frightened by it and turned their backs on us. But the few who did stick around, I swore to secrecy. Your college buddies, Iris and Ingrid, school faculty—they all respected my wishes. And on the few occasions someone did attempt to tell you…I don't know, it was weird. Like you suddenly became deaf or blind. You'd see their lips moving, but you couldn't hear the words. They'd hand you a document, and there'd be parts missing. Like a mental redaction, your subconscious was protecting you. At least, that's how Guise explained it."

My entire adolescence started to make sense. I didn't realize people knew about the random deafness. I assumed it was my little secret. Something I was afraid to tell anyone about. But here, I have psychosomatic selective hearing. This is too weird not to be true.

"What about the logistics? I live with Iris, *and* I live with Ingrid. How in the hell does that work?" When I use to go to my happy place, I'd imagine Iris's face smiling back at me. But now, Ingrid is there, too. Both are in focus. They're equals in a void.

"The way Dr. Guise puts it is the consciousness *not* being used goes into hibernation. Rarely have I ever seen you get a full night's rest. Sometimes, you're able to sleep and have the same identity when you wake up. Most of the time, though, you go into this sort of transitional state, like you're on autopilot. Kind of like sleepwalking. You get up, get dressed, and find your way back to the other home. It's been harder since you've been married. You live so far apart now. When you were younger, you kept apartments next to one another. In college, you were your own roommate."

So that's why he was never around.

"But now, you get in a car and drive across town. I get so worried about all the things that might happen. What if you were hit by a car or mugged or you simply ran out of gas? Who knows what could happen?"

I'm dazed, like I'm being forced to take the SAT's, and I didn't study.

"And the girls—they *just* went along with it? They agreed to marry a man they'd ultimately be forced to share?" I don't know if I hate them or love them for that. I can't imagine what it must be like, day-in and day-out.

"It hasn't been easy. I'll be honest. I've had my reservations. But the truth is, they both love you. Maybe more than I've ever seen four people love each other. The girls struggled for sure. But I've been there all along, helping them through the process. I gotta tell you, it's rare you see two people light up when they see one another. So, when I realized both you and Cash felt that with the girls, I knew I couldn't stand in the way. I've done everything in my power to help you boys out."

It's like I'm meeting my mother for the first time. This is the most earnest and caring I've heard her speak with me in years.

"And the girls, they know each other?"

"Yes. It's not like they're great friends. Although, if under different circumstances, they might be great friends. But yeah, this doesn't work if they don't talk."

Iris is far stronger than I ever gave her credit for.

"So, Cash…you love him?"

"Like a son. He *is* my son. As much as you. Don't get me wrong, he pisses me off with some of his bullshit. Hell, a lot of his bullshit. But, so do you. It doesn't mean I'm not going to love you both with all my heart. Call it a mother's burden."

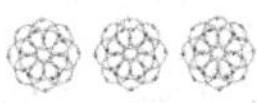

I'm so inside my head that I don't notice when Mom sits next to me. She puts an arm around my shoulder, and I'm little boy again.

The unintelligible fear stalking me throughout adolescence, the shear confusion pervading every minute of my teen years, returns. Being home-schooled was lonely, but now I know why my mother has always been so omnipresent throughout my life, and at the same time, so distant. I can't say I blame her. Like any mother, she was doing what she needed to for her child.

"What trauma?" I say it without looking at her. "Dr. Guise said I'll never be done with this unless I come to terms with this trauma. He wouldn't tell me. Said *you* should. What the hell happened to me?"

She takes a deep breath. "Rob, I don't know—"

"I want this to be over, Mom. Tell me."

She walks to the window. "What's your earliest memory?"

I don't typically think about my childhood.

"I remember coming home for Christmas. I must have been somewhere else for a long time because everyone was so excited to see me. I was about eight."

"You don't remember anything before?"

I dig into my consciousness, and I'm met with an all-consuming shiver.

"Not really. Just snap shots. A dark room. A lion…a bed?"

She takes both of my hands in hers. "Robert, I really need you to listen to me. This is not going to be easy to hear."

I know she's serious because she called me Robert.

"I am not your birth mother." Cue the ton of bricks. "You came to me at eight as a foster child. On Christmas day. That's what you're remembering. Shortly thereafter, I adopted you."

A lump swells in my throat as I labor to force words out of my mouth. All I'm able to muster is, "I don't understand."

"The truth is we don't know much about your parents. Child services found you after the police raided an underground brothel in The Bog."

My heart crashes against my ribs, and I'm having trouble breathing.

"They found you in a dark room with a single bulb, in the basement." She stops, afraid of what comes next. "They'd chained you to the bed."

The tears stream freely down her cheeks. "The man in charge sold you to men. He made them wear animal masks with you, so you couldn't recognize them. When they found you, you were covered in bedsores and malnourished. For Christ's sake, your rib cage—"

That really gets her going, and she's inconsolable. Her tears are weighted as they accumulate in spatters on the hardwood. The picture of the person she is painting holds no reality for me. She might as well be telling me about one of the women in her book club. A faceless child who suffers with each breath of his life. I want to know his pain, but he isn't me.

"We believe your mother may have been a sex slave who died while there. It's more than likely she gave birth to you at the brothel, and when she died, they chained you up. There's no telling how long they kept you there. All I know is, when you first came to live with me, you were continuing to adapt to daylight. You were like a wounded animal I nursed back to health. But before long, you latched onto me, and the idea of ever letting you go was out of the question. And I needed you the same as much as you needed me. My Robert just past. You didn't have a name when you came to me, so I named you Robert and told you he was your father."

My identity shatters like glass. Fragments breaking off in different directions, stabbing me with their truth. I'm a popping balloon. Not even my name is real.

"I'm going to be sick." I rush off to the hall bathroom, and food I didn't know was in my stomach comes back up. When I finish, I run my mouth under the sink and reluctantly return to the couch. "That's not trauma, Mom. It's sadistically systematic and deranged torture."

My whole world crashes in, imploding on itself like the projects they tore down in The Bog. Fuck. Even the words make me cringe. Disbelief battles with the inherent truth deep within. The words are a weight off my shoulders. I'm not even a real person. My name isn't Robert. My name isn't Cash.

I have no name.

I am nobody.

There's a scratch in my throat, and before I know it, I'm coughing again.

My face swells; my ears are on fire. Sharp pains pulse throughout my body. Shrapnel cuts me up inside. And my head throbs so hard my hearing and vision fade.

The last thing I remember is the smell of my mother's cookies in the next room.

Everything around me is so real. I hear, see, taste, and…I smell my mother's perfume. My real mother. It smells of lilac and jasmine. Sandalwood. I taste blood as she rocks me in her arms. She's not speaking English, but I understand her anyway.

"It'll be all right, *rebenok*. You are safe. Momma will keep you safe."

I cry into her breasts, soaking up her scent. My face hurts, like I've been punched with a bowling ball. I look up at her beauty, unconscionably young and thin. Fourteen, maybe fifteen. She smiles at me in a daze.

The room is full of half-naked, sickly women. So thin, they practically don't look human. They smoke cigarettes and stare into nothing with emotionless faces. A few of them pass out on the discolored mattresses with needles hanging out of their arms. Green stains around their nostrils.

A high window creeps dim light against the green, chipped walls, exposing the wood and wires beneath them. There is no happiness here, only my mother.

I'm being ripped out of my mother's arms, a bit older this time.

A woman screams, "Eduard, *no*. You can't take her baby. You can't take her son."

I struggle in hands as large as paws. I fight but to no avail. A large, chubby man with a cheap, dime-store lion's mask stares down at me with expressionless eyes. I claw and scratch, but the man throws me under one arm and takes me out of the room.

This is the last time I will see my mother.

Her skin is blue, and I don't catch her scent.

I'm crying in a dark room. Metal pinches my wrist, cold and stiff.

"*Momma, momma.*" I whimper. No one comes.

Bang, bang. Someone pounds on the door, and an angry voice bellows in the same language as my mother. "Stop your crying before I give you something to really cry about."

The voice shocks me to a hush. A solitary source of light comes through a sliver under the door.

I'm wearing saturated underwear. It's so cold. I shiver all the time.

A bright, naked blub swinging on a cord from the ceiling wakes me. In a small room with burgundy walls, I'm chained to a naked mattress, stained with blood, shit, and piss. The man with the lion mask grabs my free arm and shackles it to the other side of the bed forcing me face down. He wipes me off with a cold, wet rag.

The lion leads a group of men in animal masks into to the room, and they circle the bed—an elephant, a hippo, a tiger, and a chimp. Each of them takes his turn mounting me. The more I thrash and scream, the stiffer they get. By the end, I'm so exhausted that I hang limp on the brass bedposts.

This happens again and again.

I lose track of how many times the animals attack me. How many times the lion tells me, "Don't bite. Bad boys bite," as they choke me with their erections.

The taste is the worst, like gym socks and old cheese.

The screaming light wakes me again. The lion rushes in and stands me up. In a bucket to his right, he dunks a rag and smears it across my body. It stinks and stings. The bleach doesn't miss an inch of skin. I am on fire, but I'm afraid to cry. I start to block it out.

It's okay. I'll take over from here. Cash will help.

This horror continues in a cycle as I grow and mature, though I'm desperately hungry and in constant pain.

It's all I know for years on end.

In the dark, I hear a commotion. Lots of yelling, and shots fired. Two holes burst through the wall, letting in two pillars of light. Floating dust solidifies the streaks across the room.

Two policemen kick in the door and jerk away, covering their mouths and noses.

They turn on the light.

I hear one of them say, "Fucking hell."

I'm scared as I sit on a wooden bench with a blanket tossed over my shoulders.

A police station is a busy place. People rush by me in all directions.

Across the room, the two officers that found me speak to a dark-skinned woman. They're pointing at me with concerned expressions.

The noises are too loud. The light is too bright.

They give me crackers and a soda, which go untouched. I don't know what they are.

I'm curled up on my bed, now, in a room filled with beds and other little boys. A couple of them want to speak to me. But I don't know what they're saying, so I stay quiet. They don't like me, and when no one is looking, they hit me in my sleep.

I start to cough.

The dark-skinned woman catches them once and punishes them, but it doesn't stop them from doing it again.

Over and over.

Where is my Momma?

Save me, Cash.

I'm getting out of a car. Snow crunches with each step. My tiny feet make their way up to a bright-pink door. I'm being led by the dark-skinned woman. Her face is speckled and her smile large. She is nice, but I'm afraid of her. I'm sure she wants to eat me.

When the pink door opens, I'm greeted by a room full of people. A large Christmas tree stands off to the side. Decorations hang on every corner, newel post, and window frame. Everything is so loud on my eyes. Every surface shimmers. Is this place magic?

Is this where Santa lives?

A woman approaches me and extends her hand in a greeting, but I'm afraid.

She smells like my mother: lilac and jasmine.

I jump into her arms and hold on tight. I say, "Momma," and she cries.

When I come to, I'm lying on the couch with my feet up and a wet cloth on my head. It's dark outside, so I can hardly imagine how long I've been out this time.

My head is the aftermath of a pipe bomb.

I'm freezing, drenched in sweat.

"He changed? Is that a good thing?" Someone says at a distance.

"I don't know? He started changing, but then, it kept going. Like he was changing every couple of seconds. Changing faces. Lots of them I've never seen."

"What did Dr. Guise say?"

"Nothing. Just that he was on his way. He should be here soon."

"I don't know about this. Are you as scared as I am?"

"Honey, it happened right in front of me. I don't think I'll be able sleep tonight. Christ, maybe ever."

"But he's not Robert? Not Cash? It means he's coming to terms with everything. Right?"

"That's my thought, too. But who's to say?"

"I'm gonna go check on him. Make sure he's okay."

A few seconds later, Iris walks into the room carrying a bowl of steaming water. "Oh, you're up."

I look at her, and she yelps, dropping the water. It spreads quick over the hardwood.

"Iris, what's the matter?" My mom and Ingrid come rushing in and nearly slip on the spill. They follow Iris's gaze.

"Who are you? Who is that?" Ingrid holds her hands over her mouth.

"What are you talking about? It's me."

Iris looks at me like she's straining to see a magic-eye poster. "Rob?"

"Who else would it be?"

"Oh my God, honey, you look so…different." My mom is the only one brave enough to approach me.

"What do you mean?" I hurry past them to the bathroom.

In the mirror, I see a stranger. It's not me or Cash. If anything, it's a mix of the two of us. My eyes, nose, mouth; his brow line, hair, ears. I'm thinner, but not built like Cash. I can't help but run my fingers over my face. Poking and prodding.

Holy shit this is weird. But at the same time, I know exactly who I'm staring at.

My mother and two wives—I won't ever get used to saying that—gawk at me. Ingrid and I lock eyes, and it happens. A sudden rush of memories comes flooding back, as if I'd been staring at the same painting my whole life close up. But when I step back, I see so much more. Where I once only saw brush strokes, I now see landscapes.

I remember everything about Cash's life. I don't know how, but I can. I know he spied on the neighbor girl while she was changing all throughout high school. She caught him and started doing it on purpose. He lost his virginity shortly thereafter.

I remember we joined a fraternity at Ivy Pines. Pi Omega Rho. I did all the studying while he did all the partying. The guys went along with it. If for no other reason because they got a brother with the best of both worlds. I brought the grades, while he brought the ladies.

I'm remembering when he first met Ingrid at the sports bar she waitressed at. He grabbed her ass, and she slapped him. She wasn't having his chauvinist bullshit. It's what won him over. He came back the next night, a white rose in hand, and said that he was sorry.

Asked her out and turned gentleman.

I'm hit with the moment he fell in love with her. It's drastically different than when Iris and I fell in love. It's more playful. There's more laughter. He feels safe with her. I feel safe with her. As I focus on her in the mirror, back in the real world, I can't help but let a fat tear roll down my cheek.

"Cash?" Her voice is hopeful. As if her husband hasn't really died. I haven't.

In the mirror, I watch myself change into Cash. It's not painful. I don't cough. It's like flexing a muscle. I'm both of us now.

Both of us, and so, so many more.

I face her, and she rushes up, kissing me. I kiss her back but pull away.

"Hold on. Cash, yes," I say.

A smile crosses her face as she bites her bottom lip.

I look to Iris.

"But Rob, too." A spark of optimism crosses Iris' face.

As effortless as before, I flash into Rob, then back to the face they didn't recognize. "And yet, I'm neither."

I look to my mom. "I remember everything. Before I came to you, Cash's life, things I blocked out. Everything. It's like I'm a mix of both men. No. Many men. Maybe even a woman or two. But this face, here. I think this is who I really am. Who I might have been. Eduard…Edward. My real name is Edward."

"Precisely."

Dr. Guise is in the doorway, eyes bulging as he takes off his coat.

"Remarkable. The third personality wasn't new at all. It was you. The real you. The XR-21 must have fundamentally affected your genetics in ways we never considered. I need to go back and look at the data again, but it appears Robert and Cashmere are *both* false identities. Protective suits of armor to shield you from the trauma you experienced throughout your childhood. My boy, it appears you have…evolved." He says the last bit like an excited schoolboy.

My mother gives me a hug like when I was little. Her perfume has never changed.

I don't know about all that. Evolved is an aggressively optimistic word at this point. But I am whole. For the first time in my life, I'm a real person.

Before, I might not have come to that conclusion. How or why would you suspect you're merely half of an entire personality?

What I do know is that I have three women staring at me with authentic surprise and love. Each of them loves me in a completely different, yet genuine, way. One of them raised me. One of them married me. And one of them is having my baby. I didn't ask for two lives; two wives. Polygamy is the last thing I ever wanted, but it happened, and I'll need to deal with it.

Not exactly a conversation I'm looking forward to.

And we're not alone, either. There's more of us. Every day, I find a new person inside of me. Every day, I discover new ways to live, to love. We are all so different. Different ages, sexes, desires, needs.

On the up side, I'm never lonely.

On the down side, I'm always exhausted with myself.

All I know is no matter how you experience it, you can't control love. It is an unstoppable force, both irrational and uncompromising. It's painful, sour, and absurd as well as soothing, sweet, and maybe the most logical of all emotions.

So, if you are confused, join the club. We don't get it either. We'll be figuring this one out for quite a while.

What I will tell you is I love these women with all my heart.

And I'm never letting go.

X.

Few things in life are as terrifying as knowing the uncanny as fact. As a object you've seen or touched or acknowledged. When every scientific model and assumption falls on its face because of what your senses tell you, it does something to a man. Causes him to look at himself in all the ways he's avoided. It marks a point in his life where there is no coming back, no matter how unwanted or essential that juncture might be.

And it was on the occasion when the North American Great Ape, in all his pygmaean glory, found himself on the cover of *The Lakeview Gazette*. The people of the valley, emancipated by the cloud of legend, found themselves compelled to face the most contemptible of all conclusions.

The uncanny valley.

How much of themselves they recognized in the little monster's eyes.

As for Jinx Jenkins, he knew who he was and who he was not. Maybe, better than anyone in all of Green Valley. And so, he recognized the picture of the tiny, hairy beast, while sifting through the trash. He gave a hoot, saying, "I know dat boy. He ma friend."

As apt as Mr. Jenkins was to accept the beast, the rest of the valley was primed for rejection. Refusing to see the common link between themselves and the creature.

Perhaps, the greatest tragedy of all.

CIVILIZED MAN

In the depths of the Green Valley highlands, sixth degree Wilderness Scout, Pierre Abbé, tracker and student of nature, came across the legend of the Great American Ape. It surprised him as he and his troop sat around the fire, listening to the tale, to learn the people of Green Valley told stories of the shaggy beast who roamed the hills for generations.

But what surprised him more was that this horrific beast had a name.

They called it Ya'hootie.

Later that night, Pierre made his way out into the deep of the dry and lazy forest. It wasn't long before the breaking of branches and shuffling leaves alerted him to the presence of a stranger. He readied his camera, the flash on standby, and raised his lantern to discover the Great American Ape; proving Nature follows no rhyme, nor reason.

Among the no-see-ums and the pines dry with autumn, among the departed vegetation of the most torpid bronze, Pierre Abbé came face to face with a beast no larger than a young child, such as himself. It stared at him, upright, with large saucer eyes, behind a swine snout. Its long, white hair matted with leaves and soil. And when the naturalist flashed his camera, the thing's ears, pointy like a horse, perked up, it's pupils swelled, and let out a stupefied squawk.

He later informed the *Valley Gazette* that the beast was once a settler traveling west who became ill with a mysterious disease and placed alone in the woods, away from the wagon train, where he slept for a hundred years. All the while, his body changed, evolving into the shaggy midget eventually known as Ya'hootie.

When he woke, he'd been confused and afraid. No longer a man, he was now one of Nature's grander perversions. He lived in the woods, alone for fifty years, cautious of the deathly lights and preoccupied valley people. In the dry death of the forest, which rotted the leaves slowly and gave them an unbearably pungent smell, Ya'hootie had a wound in its paw.

Meanwhile, there he stood, the Pygmy Bigfoot. For an instant, in the murmur of the sleeping forest, it was as though the scout unexpectedly arrived at the truth of the matter.

The boy's snapshot of Ya'hootie was printed in the *Valley Gazette*, a candid truth revealed him swimming in wooly fur, from his elongated snout down to his large feet. His eyes were wide with the shock of the camera's flash, while his jaw was agape in a near partial smile. His rounded teeth, almost sapien in origin. There was something that made one remember their family pet.

The day the picture ran in the paper, Ethel Gunderson of the Seeder Creek Retirement Village, a grandmother of three and member of the bridge club, announced that she threw the paper in the wastebasket, "afraid of the little devil and its soulless eyes."

In the cat-infested apartment of Janice Richards, the woman came to love the beast so deeply, were he to be left with the woman for a few hours, she would surely smother him. The woman overcome by desire, pined for the unconditional love she lost when her child died, as one of her many felines decomposed behind a stack of older *Gazettes* and jars of toenail clippings. After all, it was autumn, and the world decayed all around her.

In a different home, in the town of Evergreen, little Molly Winthrop, after examining the picture of Ya'hootie, listened to her parents' astonishment of such a unique, little thing. As she was an only child, and her greatest asset was such that she was so uniquely cute and small, the fear grew within her that such an exceptional beast possessed the ability to surpass her irreplaceable status, and perhaps, even supplant her. Though she did not have the words for it at the time, the picture of the animal caused her to feel, with great trepidation, envy for the first time in her short and adorable life.

In the basement of the Cranston Funeral Home in the heart of downtown Highland Gardens, Jerry Graber, the mortician's apprentice, announced to his superior while embalming the late Robert Winters, "Look at his face. The little guy must be terrified."

"I suppose," said Thomas Cranston—unmoved, heartless, and cold. "Kind of reminds me of those dogs you see on ASPCA commercials."

"I guess," the student said.

In a proud postwar prefabricated home in the suburb of Timber Ridge, a particularly devious child said to his father over breakfast, "Imagine if I hid the hairy thing in Tina's closet. I bet she'd pee herself. Scream so loud, she'd break a mirror. I bet we could train him. I'm sure we could teach him to roll over and sit. Maybe even play dead."

The boy's last word reminded the father of a boy he knew as a child with an affinity for pyrotechnics. He'd forced fireworks into mailboxes, old refrigerators, and under cars right as the driver was about to pull away. He found a dead raccoon on the side of the road, subjected it to one of his many firecrackers and realized his true obsession with blood and gore. He blew up dead animals, always via the rear cavity, wherever he could find them.

One day in the woods, a stray dog happened upon their playground, and the boy lured him over with the promise of a bologna sandwich. The father simply watched as the boy violated the dog with a string of black cats, lighting the fuse. He'd never told anyone about that day, of the carnage, doing his best to forget it altogether. But he recognized the same look in his son's eyes as he'd seen in his friend's.

The father remembered this again while hunched over the sink, shaving the white hair from his face. What did it mean to be a man?

With so many different origins, all men appeared to funnel into the same basic construct. But what was it that truly made a man happy, beyond the false successes of work and of home?

Where did a man's true joy come from?

Was any happiness a man felt not in some way tied to a predetermined sense of duty?

The happiest man he'd ever seen was a vagrant riding the tram, giggling and hooting to himself.

The blatant future awaiting his son made him nick himself with his blade; a trickle of blood dripping from his chin, staining the murky white water with a gentle red.

He stared into the face of every boy that ever grew to become a true man.

And he found himself terrified to his core, watching the water change to ever-darker shades of red. Thus, he watched his son, uneasy, for the rest of the day as he waged war with his friends in the piles of leaves on their back lawn.

"I must take him hunting. Maybe buy him his first rifle," he said. He dressed his boy in camouflage and thrust a weapon into his hand, as if masculinity were a thing that could be taught, and thus, refine the boy's deeper nature.

Adamantly producing in his son and in himself something truly primal in solely the way a human could be.

For it was staring into the basin of blushed water that he witnessed his own face slowly transform into that of Ya'hootie, negating the insurmountable expanse of evolution. And with decades of experience passed down to him from all the fathers that came before him, he ascertained this was a Sunday in which it was pertinent to initiate his budding son.

In a posh and spacious apartment in Lakeview's Jefferson Park district, a family sat around determining the true height and weight of the Ape-Man in reference to the family Collie. As they toyed with the measuring tape bemusing the things true nature, they came to an astonishing discovery and insight: His size was more infinitesimal than any of them could have previously contemplated. And each of them wanted to have this bearded thing for themselves. The chewing desire to own the precious and abominable little man ate into their most primordial needs as civilized peoples. This travesty of a beast endured for so long, alone amongst the trees; surely, it wanted to be owned. What animal didn't wish to be taken in and cared for? To be kept and paraded about. To be loved without reason, even after all romance was faded by time.

"I'm willing to bet if we had him here, it would take the blame away from me," said the father as he watched his football game in the next room. "Somehow, everything in this house gets blamed on me."

"Don't be so defensive, George," said the mother.

"Dad, do you think if we built it a house in the back yard, he would live in it?" their oldest son, twelve, asked.

Considering all the other animals the boy brought into the house as pets, the mother cringed and returned to the story.

"I suppose so, sport," he said over his shoulder, refusing to tear his eyes from the television. "We might even be able to train him to serve your dear old dad a beer during the game."

"*George*. If you want a beer so bad, all you have to do is ask." The mother's face tensed.

"You've got to admit," the father said, defending himself, "the wooly little beast is one of a kind. I could put a jersey on him and teach him to dance at touchdowns. And yes, if you're offering, I'd love another beer."

And what about the rare and bushy beast?

Meanwhile, in the deepest part of the arbor preserve, while face-to-face with the tiny scout, the rare beast felt a reminiscence toward the boy lingering deep within his DNA. The walking enigma held up its hand, exposing a cleanly naked palm, white and Caucasian.

After a time, the boy was able to decipher a kind of language between himself and the beast interpreting particular sounds and gestures, and thus, was able to ask questions.

Ya'hootie said it was a fulfillment unlike any other to live as one with Nature, his bride, and his dear friends, the trees. Because—and the boy was only able to determine this from the look in the beast's face—because knowing one's true place in this world so truly pleasant. The boy, dumbfounded, scratched at his bug bites.

"Well I'll be...," said an old man gumming his runny eggs and toast at Johnny's Diner in the open lands along Main Street. He shook the paper slack in his hand. "Well I'll be...I will say this—Nature is one crazy broad."

And from a booth in the corner of the diner, Nature, in her infinite wisdom, chuckled.

XI.

Americans are the laziest, most entitled collection of human beings the world has ever produced. This much was always clear to our dear Master Jenkins. But, as dilatory as Americans might have been, it always baffled him why anyone in Lakeview took a cab. What with the accessibility the SkyTram offered; a person was able to get anywhere in the city with merely a few line changes. More cost effective for sure. And you weren't beholden to the navigational acumen of a person who'd likely just moved to the city.

These weren't Jinx's views exactly, but rather a summation of the incoherent ramblings of the bum. He spotted a young woman exit a Ryde car. She was particularly attractive and went into a watering hole. The bar's owner, on occasion, charitably shared the tail end of a bottle with the pariah.

In the car, the driver's eyes followed the woman all the way into the bar before noticing something in his backseat. He stretched to retrieve it, gazed at the item for a minute, then to the bar, back at the item, and placed it in his glove box.

Sometimes in life, we come into contact with people we don't want to let go of. And in those cases, often the best we can come by is a memento to keep their memory alive.

ROULETTE

There's a lot you can learn about yourself in those long moments of anticipation before you see someone you're in love with. I hadn't seen her in months, and like that, we were suddenly meeting for dinner. When I saw her finally walk through the doors, my heart crashed headlong into a brick wall. A little dizzy, every word I knew ceased to exist. The hostess took her coat, and she made her way around the partition. And when she came into full view, everything in my life changed.

Fuck that, I'm getting way ahead of myself. Let's start from the beginning.

I fucking hate driving. Each minute spent behind the wheel of a car is a minute wasted. A minute I can't get back. A minute I die a little. So why did I become a driver for Ryde? Didn't have a lot of choices, now did I? Parents cut me off a couple years back after I graduated with a B.A. in B.S. I don't blame them. After all, that's what you're supposed to do when kids grow up. Push 'em out of the nest, and see if they've been paying attention to the flying lessons. But what about the ones who had shitty instructors?

My parents never told me a thing about money. We didn't talk about it. It showed a lack of class. One day, it was there, and the next, not even the stale scent of a dollar left in my wallet. That's not true. I did have some money left over from graduations, my first communion, savings bonds—things like that. So, I did what I trusted to be a good idea and invested it all into starting a food delivery company with my best friend-slash-roommate.

You might have heard of it, ChowNow.

How was I supposed to know he'd steal the company right out from under me? After that, he sold the company to BigCorp and laughed all the way to the bank. So, why'd I take a job driving sad sacks all over Green Valley if I hate driving? I couldn't stand working for a company that I started yet barely made minimum wage plus tips. Besides, they said it paid well, and fast, and my revulsion didn't seem to matter when I couldn't pay for cable.

But as much as I want to bitch about driving for Ryde, if it weren't for the job, I'd have never met the love of my life, Robbie.

Short for Roberta.

A former senator's daughter turned Miss Michigan turned Sniff junkie turned homeless car dweller turned prostitute turned lesbian turned born-again something or other. When I met her, she was working as a bar tender at a Staph-infected punk bar that doubled as a Lakeview Leviathans' hang out on game day. But that's not where I first saw her. I first laid eyes on her as a passenger. Picked her up in Aviation Park, a beach community down by the lakefront.

I pulled up and hit the series of buttons on the Ryde app to let her know I'd arrived. Should've known what I was getting myself into when I waited for ten minutes before she opened the front door. Her profile didn't have a picture. All I had was the name Robbie. So, when a beautiful buxom blonde popped into my back seat, I double checked. "Uh,…Robbie?"

"Yeah, that's me."

"Sorry. There was no picture, and I like to check—"

"Sure. I'm actually running really late to work. Do you mind if we just go?"

I pulled out and merged into traffic. In this job, I get cut off mid-sentence all the time. You'd be amazed at how shitty people are when they want to blame someone for something that's their own fault. Like being late or not knowing where they're going. I try not to let it bother me, though.

I simply imagine them getting out of my car and getting hit by a bus or falling off a cliff or getting mugged when they get to their door. If they really wanted to get somewhere so quick, they shouldn't have taken ten minutes to get out to the fucking car.

But Robbie's case was different. Something in her raspy voice. A hint of desperation. A plea for help. And those crystal blue eyes staring back at me in the rearview. Fuck—even the memory of them makes my chest cave.

She was a cigarette come to life. Sleek and slim and sexy in all the ways you're too afraid to admit your attracted to; and at the same time full of chemicals and bitterness and addiction in a way where if I wasn't careful, I knew would be the death of me.

I did my best to make small talk with her as she dumped out the contents of her life on my back seat and started sifting through them for various makeup products, tampons and pill bottles, eyelash curlers and tiny bags of coke, a strip of condoms, and a tiny rabbit-shaped vibrator. She also had a giant wad of bills tied off with a rubber band. Most women in her situation would have quickly scooped up their more personal items back into the bag.

Not Robbie.

She let them sit on the seat next to her as if they were sharing the ride. She told me she was from Michigan, and she was a bartender, and I shouldn't get any ideas while she perked up her tits in the low-cut tank top—she was a lesbian. This last part was only half-true. But I didn't find that out until later.

"Not that it's any of my business, but that's quite a bit of money to be carrying around."

She glanced at the hefty wad. "I don't have a bank account. Avoiding creditors. You know, if you don't pay your debts after twenty years they get expunged. I'm just riding it out. Don't pay for anything I can't use cash for."

"That doesn't sound right."

"A friend of mine told me about it."

"Did you at least research if they were right?"

"He's trustworthy. He knows all about credit and debt and shit."

That was Robbie in a nutshell. Willing to change her entire life on a load of bullshit.

Before she exited, she took note the pair of fuzzy die hanging from my rearview with the Leviathans' logo on it. As she put her life back in her bag, she said, "You know, my bar. It's a Leviathans' bar on Sundays. Big crowd. You should stop by some time."

I told her I would. Probably a little too energetically from the way she smiled.

I dropped her off at the Come Bucket, where she worked. As she twirled to go inside, her hip-huggers made her ass look like a pillow I wanted to rest my head on and never wake up from. The small of her back was exposed as she tied her flannel off above her navel. I full-on expected her to be sporting a regrettable tramp stamp—she had other tattoos—but her lower back was clean. Two dimples perched right above her ass, and the tiny blond hairs glistened in the afternoon sun.

Fuck me, if that wasn't the hook that caught me.

Right before she passed through the front door of the bar, she gazed over her shoulder, eyes grinning.

In my rearview, something shiny caught my eye, a memento she'd missed from her bag. A keychain. A miniature roulette wheel with a tiny silver pebble, which jumped about on the inside.

I told myself she left it behind on purpose, convinced the only thing to do was return it come Sunday.

Only Sunday was five days away.

I put the roulette wheel in my glove box and drove off to get my next fare at the Columbian Circus.

For the rest of the week, I kept it in my pocket. When I was alone, I smelled it for any remaining hint of *Essence de Robbie*. Spinning the keychain on my finger, the little ball spun in a chaotic flurry. Where it landed, a gamble—just like the girl. I'd close my eyes and imagine her getting ready in my back seat. It always ended up with her stripping off her top and inviting me into the back, where we attacked each other's mouths and let our bodies fall into place.

Even then, I knew she was lying about the whole lesbian thing. Clearly a self-defense mechanism to scare away would-be perverts.

I considered myself in the rearview.

I was certainly a pervert.

I've never anticipated a Sunday the way I did that one. All week long, I daydreamed about the mysterious woman from my car.

Robbie. Robbie, Robbie, Robbie.

The more I said her name in my head, the less of a male connotation I got from it. It was as if the name were created for her and only her. As I parked my car and walked up to the Come Bucket, I couldn't help but wonder how much I'd built this girl up in my head.

When I saw her again, would she ever meet my expectations?

My eyes took a second to adjust to the dark room. Concrete floors and high-top tables. The bar was to the right, rimmed with rusting steel and a mirrored back wall. The other patrons faced the same direction, so I spun around, and next to the door was a short, elevated stage with a projector screen playing the Leviathans game. Still in the first quarter. Second and six. 12:42 left.

A running back caught a screen pass and broke the ankles of the defense.

The crowd erupted in hysterics. He spun and twirled, hurdled and threw a stiff arm.

"Go, go, go, go…" people around me shouted.

At the twenty, the ten, the five…

"I know you!"

I turned to see Robbie behind the bar, her hair in two loose blond braids, a white Leviathans t-shirt with strategic cuts around the belly and cleavage.

"Hey…" I pretended not to remember her name right away. "Robbie, right?"

"You came." She made no pretense as to remembering my name.

"I did. Puck. Like, *A Midsummers Nights Dream.*" I reached in my pocket and felt the roulette wheel.

"Well, Puck, what can I get 'cha?"

I pulled an empty hand out of my pocket. “Bach Light. A pitcher.”

She got me the beer, and I found a place at the bar where I could see the screen. But the more I told myself to pay attention to the game, the more I couldn’t stop looking at Robbie. She was exactly how I remembered her. Better even, considering the lighting. Holy hell, who in their right mind could concentrate on football at a time like this? With a masterpiece of the fairer sex like Robbie in the same room.

Down the bar, she flirted *at* another customer, shooting off her fatal smile, flashing those amazing blue eyes. And every so often, she’d look in my direction. That’s when I knew. She liked me. To what extent, I wasn’t sure, but she liked me. Her face flushed, and her teeth bit her bottom lip. Our gazes connected, and she looked away. Caught in the act.

Showing your cards a little too early, Robbie.

Eventually, she came down and struck up a conversation with me. Certainly nothing of consequence, so I won’t go into it. All that’s important is once the Leviathans won the game and people slowly drifted out, I made my move and asked her if she’d like to get a bite to eat sometime.

All you need to know is that she said yes.

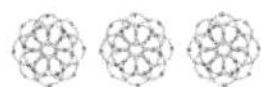

I picked her up at her place. Easy ‘cause I already knew where she lived. Once again, I waited outside for a good ten minutes. When she came out, she looked like a business professional. Like a sexy secretary. She was a chameleon like that. She wore a charcoal skirt and a thick-nit turtleneck sweater. Red, the color your finger becomes when you wrap a string around it too tight.

I realized I’d forgotten to take a breath when she opened the car door. She had that effect on people. I inhaled a great plume of her perfume and felt a little dizzy. She was covered up, showing as little skin as possible, so this wasn’t exactly a romantic date. But the color of the dress and the perfume meant it wasn’t entirely off the table.

I took her to one of my favorite sushi places down by the water. It overlooked the lake, and we watched as the sun tucked itself in under the horizon.

Her roulette wheel hid in my pocket.

I ordered the baked scallops for us both, and she introduced me to soft shell crab. She seemed different, like she wasn't sure of how to act without a few feet of mahogany between us. Months later, I found out it was the first date she'd ever been on where she wasn't weaseling something out of them.

"You wanna get a drink? I think it might help break the ice."

"Do you like sake," she asked.

"Yeah, sure I do."

She flagged down the waiter and ordered two bottles of something in Japanese. She fucking spoke Japanese. And not that I know anything about the language, but it sounded like she knew what she was doing.

A minute later, the waiter brought back two tiny bottles and little cups. Until then, the only sake I'd drank was the hot, shitty rice urine you get in a sake bomb. But this was nice. Milky in color. Sort of tasted like bananas.

With each bite of sushi, we took another shot.

And the more we drank, the more she opened up.

"I like you, Puck. You're fun."

Told ya she liked me.

"I like you, too. You've got me on my toes."

"Manny's gonna like you."

"Is that your cat or something?"

"No. Manny's my boyfriend."

The words echoed all around me. This happened to me before. A woman going out with me when she full well knew she had a boyfriend. Usually, they waited for me to make a move before kicking me in the jewels. Why they did it, I never understood. Maybe, I was revenge or a fling, or they simply didn't understand no man is actually their friend.

If you are a woman, and relatively attractive, every man you know has fantasized about having gratuitously raunchy sex with you. Even the sweet ones. Hell, especially the sweet ones. They're the dirtiest dicks of all.

My boyfriend...

Fuck.

"Your boyfriend?"

This was where I was supposed to get up and stiff her with the bill. Where she would call me a horny fuck and all men want the same thing, blah, blah, fuckidy blah.

Well, I didn't.

I know—self-respect much, Puck?

You say that now. But had you seen the way she stared into your soul with those shiny sapphires, you'd stay quiet, too. I don't care what sex you are. Simply being around Robbie made me feel like someone.

Someone important.

"Yeah, you'll like him." *Doubt that.* "He works in commercial real estate. He's got his own company."

"He's cool with you being out with me?"

"Sure. Told him I was going out with a *friend* from the bar."

And there, I had it. My status: friend. Nothing more.

But I figured even a friend got to spend time with her, so why not give it a shot. I'd played the long game before. I'd never come out on top, but I was certainly familiar with the sport. The odds weren't in my favor, but it was a gamble I was willing to take.

After sushi, we went back to her place where I continued to hope at some point she'd forget about this Manny guy and tell me to take her on the kitchen sink. Instead, she showed me her snake. Percy, a boa constrictor. It was feeding time. So, she grabbed a live mouse from another tank and plopped it in with the serpent.

She urged me down onto the carpet next to her to watch as Percy slowly made his way to the corner where the rodent was desperately clawing for freedom. Even animals as simple as these know what roles they took on in any given situation. No pretense. Simply what *was* and *was not*. The truth.

As we waited for the snake to make his move, I couldn't help but focus on how close we were. Our fingertips separated by a hair. I could smell alcoholic bananas on her breath.

I saw how much makeup she'd caked on for our dinner—for me.

She looked at me. At my mouth. My lips.

My heart felt like an anvil determined to fall.

I leaned in a little.

She did the same.

And right as our mouths where about to lock, Percy struck his pray.

I jumped, startled by the ferocious nature of the animal behind the glass. "Whoa. Holy fuck. Shit. Dammit."

Robbie leapt back, startled by my reaction, and laughed so hard she cried.

The moment was over.

Fleeting as the life of the mouse, slowly being swallowed whole.

Eventually, I did meet Manny. And yeah, he was a pretty cool guy. A little pudgy and a bit on the showy side. But for the most part, a decent guy. I hated him all the more for it.

He knew why I was there, but he acted as though I wasn't a threat, which in turn made me no threat at all. She wanted money and stability, the one thing he had and I didn't.

But it didn't stop me from hanging around Robbie every chance I could, a busty blond enigma. We'd take long drives on the Main Street expressway around Green Valley as she told me about her fucked-up family, and I pieced together the story that lead her to Lakeview.

She'd been forced to play the perfect daughter of a state senator, always keeping up appearances. Not until she was at the Miss USA pageant, representing Michigan, did she use coke for the first time. It wasn't long before she was skipping school and going down on her father's campaign manager for a bump. Her parents caught them together, and soon after, her mother kicked her out of her house. She drove as far as her car would take her and hitchhiked the rest of the way to Lakeview. She didn't have any money, so she paid with her mouth everywhere she went. She found an abandoned car and lived out of the back. From cocaine, she moved on to Molly; from Molly to meth; from meth to heroin; heroin to Sniff; until one night she overdosed in the motel bathroom of a john. He called for an ambulance and split before it arrived. She spent a couple of years in and out of rehab, but not because she was getting clean. Because she was working for a dealer who targeted "customers in free agency."

Her hair was dyed every color of the gay flag, and she'd even shaved her head into a Mohawk. I didn't believe her at first, but she showed me the picture on her license. Sure enough, she had a pitch-black fan of hair, striped down the center, and a spiteful grin on her face, as if saying, "This is gonna piss off my dad so much."

Then, the story turned cold. She never talked about how she traveled from there to here. Anytime I broached the subject, she'd change the story to something off topic like, "Did I ever tell you 'bout the time I did it with all five members of *Terry Bell and the Glitter Critters*?" And I'd fall for it, a dog chasing an invisible ball.

Because seriously, who doesn't want to hear that story?

But despite her redirections, she always tensed up. Whatever she went through was traumatic as fuck. For an instant, she relived it before returning to the sly-smiled vixen I'd become enamored with.

I eventually found a second job working for FaceSpace as a content manager in BigCorp Tower. In simplest terms, I became a smut censor. Porn police. I continued to drive for Ryde. But at least, I was on my way to proving to Robbie I could have a normal job like anyone else.

Looking for some extra cash, she was hired a few weeks after me. Truth was, she wanted to hang out with me during the day. And since my new job was taking up all my time, she figured she'd come to me. All day long, we'd sit at cubicles next to each other, cracking jokes and going for long lunches.

She favored scrolling through the pictures and videos of people degrading each other in the most disgusting ways imaginable, and announcing, "Done it. Done it. That one, too. Yup. What the fuck? That's a thing? Oh, I see it now. Yeah, definitely done that."

It wasn't long until we were both fired for slacking off. As a goodbye present, we infected the founder, Joe's, homepage with a nasty virus that brought down the entire site for a few days. There's nothing quite as satisfying in this life as fucking up your workplace on your last day.

The job sucked anyway.

And I still had Ryde to fall back on. As for Robbie, she found a job tending bar later that afternoon.

At some point in our shenanigans, she's moved in with Manny, where she'd gone brunette. She was cryptic about why. She looked so damn hot as a blond. But it likely had to do with the dealer she worked for during her rehab days.

"Is everything okay? Are you safe?"

"Yeah, I'm just taking precautions." At that, she rushed to the kitchen, grabbed a pair of scissors, and hurried to the bathroom. I followed her in.

Unpleasant thoughts of her limp on the floor, bleeding to death forced themselves on me.

But when I rounded the corner, she was using them on her hair.

"You know they have places that do that professionally?"

"Yeah, for a tit and a twat. You ever seen how much they charge for a women's haircut? I don't have that kind of cheddar laying around."

I sat on the toilet doing my best to give her pointers on how to even it out. When she was done she looked like she'd humped a light socket. But fuck me if she didn't pull that shit off. Girl could make a duct tape ball-gown look couture.

After her DIY haircut, we headed to the Come Bucket. She'd left some things there the night before when she'd gotten drunk and finger fucked a girl in the bathroom. The bar was closed when we arrived, but she had keys.

It was like one of my fantasies, playing out in perfect cinematic fashion. Alone in the bar, we'd get drunk on stolen booze and fuck on top of the sealed mahogany. It seemed like the perfect moment to make a move. To this day, I'm not sure why I didn't. I'm sure fear was in there somewhere. But regardless, all we ended up doing that afternoon was playing the nudy eye-spy game at the bar.

It was like that, with me, for Robbie. She'd give me these amazing openings to make a move. But for whatever reason, I never followed through. I assume that's why she stayed with me. She knew she was safe. But at the same time, I can only imagine how confused she must have been at the doughy-bodied nobody rejecting her advances.

Eventually, she broke up with Manny. But within a few days, she was back in a relationship with some douchebag named Steve. She told me she found him on SugarDaddy.com. He was a lawyer, and she'd been writing him for a couple of weeks. He agreed to pay her rent in return for being his plaything and arm candy.

He did *not* like me.

Not in the least.

In fact, I overheard them fighting once about me.

"You're fucking him. That's clear. I just want to know what else you're doing with him."

"Puck? Are you serious? Gross. He's like my brother. 'Sides, I don't think he could find my pussy if I gave him a fucking map."

That was a kick to the junk, but I acknowledged a hint of disappointment in her voice.

"Whatever. Say what you want. I've seen how you two look at each other. It's like I'm in a guest role on the Puck and Robbie show."

"I said, we're friends."

"Guys can't be friends with girls. Especially not ones like you. At best, a guy is friend-*ly*. But in the back of his mind, he's always picturing you naked and fantasizing about you in different positions. Don't play dumb with me. You *know* what I'm talking about."

Steve wasn't around long.

It came to a head when Robbie invited me to Pureza Island, right off the coast of Lakeview, on what was supposed to be a romantic weekend with Steve. She also invited a cousin, Julie, she'd never mentioned. During the day we got hosed at all the local watering holes, playing drunken mini golf, smoking some weed with the tourists, and singing karaoke at night. When it was time for bed, she and Steve started another row, while I lay on the pullout couch in the next room. They screamed for about an hour before she came out of the room in a huff and slammed the bedroom door. Five minutes later, Steve left through a sliding door into the cobbled stone streets.

She didn't ask me if she could share my bed, she just slipped in, wearing skimpy panties and an old tee shirt—the one I'd given her off my back when a drunk at the Come Bucket vomited on her halter top.

"You still have that?"

"Yeah. It's what I sleep in every night."

A memento.

Part of me wanted to tell her about the roulette wheel I kept stashed away in my bag. But the black streaks of eyeliner running down her cheeks, told me it wasn't the right time.

"God. What a fucking dick. You know he's only able to get it up when I call him Daddy. Seriously, what a perv. Wants me to pretend I'm his daughter."

I put my hand on her shoulder and rubbed her back. "He's quite certainly a cock gobbler. I mean, Manny was whatever, but Steve—I don't get why you felt you needed to go to SugarDaddy.com. I don't know why you feel like you've gotta fuck some old dude for his money. Robbie, you're better than that. You might not think so. But when I see you, all I know is my chest gets tight, it's hard to breath, and I've never been happier in my damn life. I'm not saying, 'Be with me, not with him,' or something as fucking dramatic. All I'm saying is you deserve better. I wish you'd stop hating yourself."

Her tears stopped, and she gave me a nubile smile. The kind a kid gives a parent after they've been talked out of running away to the tree house. She scooted closer and touched my arm. "Spoon with me?"

The next morning, I found her beside me on the pull out. To this day, I've never slept so easy with someone else in the bed. We didn't have sex, but what we shared was so much more intimate. When we returned to shore, she and Steve broke up. I'd say the final straw came when she found Steve and Julie making out on the ferry home. Robbie retaliated by whipping a fifth of rum at the fucker's skull.

Suddenly tight on money again, she moved into a spare room with her boss from the Come Bucket. It was just temporary; until she got back on her feet, which worked out great for me. Her boss' place was two blocks from mine.

I figured the stars were finally aligning for me. I was going to tell her how I felt and what I wanted. I grabbed her roulette wheel and walked over after my Ryde shift one night. My version of a bouquet; only, I felt it held more meaning.

But when I arrived, once again, she had a boyfriend she met at work.

I never met him. His name was Ian or Ethan or Fuckface. Something like that. All she told me was he converted "meat-eating murderers" into raw vegans. Soon, all I ever heard from her was how terrible I was for eating a deli sandwich. "Do you have any idea what goes into bologna? Do you know what they do to cows and pigs at the slaughterhouse? Did you know there's at least five percent rat shit in every hot dog?"

Those were the dark days. The girl I'd fallen for was criticizing everything I put in my mouth, and it wore on me.

"No thanks, I don't eat chips anymore. They're cooked with prisoner animal byproduct."

I saw Robbie less and less.

At its worst, I didn't hear a word from Robbie for about two months. She and whoeverthefuck she was dating at the time were getting pretty serious. She stopped coming by the Come Bucket on Sundays. I wish I could say I was innocent in the matter. But the truth is, I'd gotten into a fight with her about being vegan. She'd gotten so judgy, and the last thing I needed was to be converted to some politically-minded diet. So, I called her a cunt.

I regretted it the instant it slipped past my lips.

But what was said was said, and she blocked me on everything from my cell phone to FaceSpace. She was a child like that sometimes. Flying off the handle and going for the most extreme option. But, I didn't blame her. In retrospect, she was simply concerned for my health. I think, secretly, she might have been pushing me into a respectable shape so she could actually date me—but that's conjecture.

I'd all but written off my relationship with Robbie as over, when she texted me, *Sorry.*

She followed it up with a sad face emoji.

Whatever ill will I held was long past.

I found the roulette wheel and spun it.

We decided to meet up later in the week.

When I arrived at Robbie's, she was in the kitchen with a brand-new juicer—her newest fad. Apparently, chewing became too much of a burden. She was still vegan. Only now, she had the added benefit of carrying her meal with her everywhere she went in a water bottle.

"Want me to make you one?"

"Is this your way of making me a home-cooked meal?"

"Suck a dick." And like that, it was as if we hadn't skipped a beat.

She finished her liquid dinner while we watched a shitty reality show she was addicted to. She didn't have any solid food, so she offered me a beer and poured herself a brimming glass of white wine.

When all that was left was the sediment stuck to the sides of the cup, she stood up and told me to follow her to her room. I didn't think much of it. I'd been in her room before. But she told me to come sit with her on her bed this time.

As if she wanted to share something with me.

A thing more intimate than she'd ever offered in her life.

Her black yoga pants were painted on her hips and ass, and with no bra, her nipples poked through my old tee shirt. The bed was vast. King, I think. Point is, there was plenty of space, but she made it a point to sidle up real close to me.

Her chilled skin felt soft and silky.

I was about to lean in and kiss her when she said, "I've got something I want to show you."

She pulled a large scrapbook from a bookshelf at the front of the bed. Pictures of her as a little girl in pageant gowns and sparkle makeup stared up at me. Her hair was still bright blond and done up in an impossible amount of tiny, manufactured ringlets. As she flipped the pages, she posed for official photos with her mother and senator father; a picture of her crazy sister; her posing on the hood of her first car—an antique, cherry-red Thunderbird. With each page, we advanced through her life, revealing to me what I'd only imagined.

And with every new picture, it was like she shed another piece of clothing, until we arrived at her passing on her pageant crown.

At that moment, she was truly naked to me for the first time. A look of nostalgia hung on her face as she gazed back in time, the corners of her mouth yearning for simpler times.

She closed the book and climbed over me, putting the book away. On another shelf, she found a homemade VHS tape and popped it into her antique VCR. Technologically behind, she always said, "My shit ain't broke, so why replace it."

Robbie plopped back in bed and edged close to me again.

Squiggly lines populated the screen as the tracking kicked in. A title page came up: Roberta Lynn Stevens, Miss Michigan 2008. The film cut to a montage of her many highlights while holding her throne. A white sash and tiara became fixtures in each shot. She was on a fishing boat, reeling in a fighting trout; she was at a children's hospital reading to a group of children with naked heads and sunken eyes; she sat elevated in the back seat of her Thunderbird as she waved to the crowd…

"Robbie, why are you showing me this?"

"Because I want you to see it."

"Why?"

"I don't show this stuff to anyone. Manny never saw this stuff. Definitely not Steve. Nor do I think they'd give a shit." She paused for a second, choosing her words with precision for the first time since the pageant stage. "You're really important to me, Puck. I wanted to share this part of me with you. Give you something I'd never given anyone else."

Her face reddened, and I swore she might cry.

She downed the rest of her glass of wine, searching for courage. She sat up, stretching her arms and back, poking out her tits with a yawn. "I'm gonna get another drink. Want one?"

I followed her back to the kitchen where she filled her glass to the brim again, finishing off the bottle of wine. She handed me another beer, and we sat back on the couch. I'll be honest, you could hold my feet over hot coals—I wouldn't be able to tell you what the fuck we talked about. All I know is, before I was half way done with my beer, she was scrounging for the last few drops of pinot to leg their way down the side of the glass.

"I'm feeling a little gross. Think I'm gonna take a shower." She said it abruptly. Right after I'd been talking about wanting a family someday. Something along those lines.

With each step she took, she pulled off different layers of clothing and let them fall behind her. She unclasped her bra and gave me the same smile over her shoulder she'd given me when I dropped her off at the bar the first time. She was stark naked before she rounded the corner to the bathroom.

The water came on, trickling against the curtain.

I sat paralyzed on the couch. This was it. She was inviting me to join her.

Wasn't she?

Or was she so drunk she didn't realize what she was doing?

She *was* drunk.

Did I want to be with her like that?

After all, I was drunk.

What did it matter?

A swirl of desires and excited panic surged as I strained to will myself off the couch and into her shower. This was everything I ever wanted.

So why did I leave?

It felt wrong. Like a boy peeping in on the girl's locker room or a kid walking in on their parents in bed.

The whole walk home, all I wanted was to burst in on her, letting my tongue find its way. But my feet kept moving forward, away from Robbie.

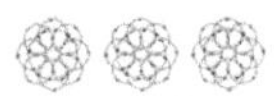

Seven months passed, and I didn't hear a word from her. Pretty sure I'd fucked things up forever. I wasted through my days picking people up and carting them off to work or the bar or wherever the fuck it was they spent their miserable existences. I'd be driving, zoned out, running my fingers over the roulette wheel, obsessing over that night and how I could have—should have—bet it all on black. But, down deep I knew I'd done the right thing. Call it drunkard's intuition. One way or another, I knew it was for the best.

One night, right as I was clocking off, an icon on my FaceSpace popped up with six unread messages. They were all from Robbie over the progression of the past five months. I felt like my stomach fell out my ass, my heart forgot what it was doing, and my hands went clammy.

She'd been struggling to get a hold of me since the day after that night. The messages started out with an apology, then confusion, then annoyance, and finally venomous, spiteful rage. She'd dropped her phone in the toilet the night I walked out on her and lost all her contacts. The sole way she knew how to get a hold of me was through FaceSpace.

But who the *fuck* checked their FaceSpace messages on the reg?

Not me. I was hardly on it anymore.

I wrote her back, explaining the situation and how I never meant for any of this to happen. That had she just walked over like a person—a normal goddamn person—we could have avoided all this. I told her that I wanted nothing more than to see her again. That I missed her more than I'd ever missed anyone or anything in my entire life, and yadda yadda, a bunch more fluffy heartfelt bullshit like that. At the end, I asked her—no fuck that—I pleaded with her to meet with me for dinner.

An hour later, I received her response. *Yes.*

We met at the sushi restaurant from our first real date. I arrived early and ordered two bottles of the banana stuff and her favorite, soft shell crab. I sat so I could see the door. She was late, as usual—the girl was late to her own birth, by three weeks.

I polished off an entire bowl of edamame by myself. When I'd given up hope, she walked in, spotted me at my table and waved from behind the hostess' partition.

The host helped her with a large pea coat, and as it was pulled from her, she shed a layer of armor.

She rounded the corner, and there it was.

Plain as day.

A baby bump. She was pregnant.

She wore a guilty look on her face as she approached the table. Like she'd been caught stealing a cookie. Even with motherhood looming, she would always be the eternal little girl. Her eyes down, only peeking up at me long enough to see where she was going. She sat down quietly.

"So…"

"Yeah…"

"How many months?"

"Seven."

I don't know much about pregnancy, but the tiny bulge did not look like it was seven months. She was scarcely showing.

"So, right after I last saw you?"

"Actually, I think it happened that night. After you left, I called Josh over, and we…"

"Right." Josh? That was his name. Fuck, I knew I didn't like him. This merely confirmed it. Never met a Josh I liked. You can't trust 'em. "And, is he aware?"

"Yeah. He wants me to get rid of it. But I don't. I want it. Unlike anything I've ever wanted in my life. I wish I could explain it better, but it just…it feels right."

I gestured at the bottle of sake and the sushi in front of her. "Guess you're not gonna be needing these."

I grabbed the bottle and raw fish and ordered her some tea and chicken teriyaki instead. In Japanese no less—thank you very much.

She broke a smile for a second but sank into herself again.

"So…seven months? Robbie, I don't mean to be forward, but shouldn't you be showing more?"

"Typically, yeah. The doctor says it was because of my diet. I kept juicing and eating vegan. And while that's healthy for me, it's not exactly the best thing for a baby. They've got me on a bunch of vitamins and meds to get the little guy up to a good size."

"Little guy? It's a boy?"

"Yeah." She smiled. This time, it wasn't sheepish. Like she really meant it. "Atticus. You know, like *To Kill a Mockingbird*. I wanted to name him after a literary character, like you. Hope you don't mind."

I wasn't sure what to say. It was endearing. But under all the crazy layers of subtext, it was like she was proposing something to me. She wanted me to be the kid's dad. She wanted me to raise some Joshua-fuck's baby with her. She never asked it, but it was implied.

I deliberated about it for all of half a second.

"Course not. I'm honored."

After dinner, I asked her if I could touch her belly.

She raised an eyebrow and said, "Was wondering when you were gonna ask."

Robbie lifted up her blouse and showed me the bump that became so overtly present throughout dinner. It was small and troubling.

I considered all the things that could have resulted in this baby being so undersized. God knows what havoc she'd done to her body with drugs and alcohol. The stretches of malnutrition when she was homeless. And certainly, this bullshit vegan/juicing thing she'd become a disciple of.

But, as soon as my hand touched her belly and felt her soft skin, it stopped being the idea of a baby and started being an actual, living person growing inside her.

Call me a bastard, but later that night when I was laying in bed, part of me realized why I didn't follow her into the shower. Part of me, way the fuck down in my subconscious knew this was going to happen. And part of me was ecstatic that it wasn't mine.

That instant, I felt like a shit.

How selfish can a person be?

I decided that night to take the scariest gamble of my goddamned life. I'd tell her I love her, I'd help her through this, and I wanted to raise the baby with her.

I'd never been more unsure of anything in my life. But, unlike the night she'd invited me into the shower, this felt right.

I read as many parenting blogs as I could find. I took on extra hours behind the wheel. I even bought a few books. Josh might have fathered this kid, but I was gonna be its dad. All I cared about was that Atticus and Robbie were cared for. It didn't matter if we were romantic or not. Atticus was so much more important than any personal sexual needs.

Then, a week later, she called me in tears. I was checking out at the supermarket. I couldn't make out what she was saying, but I knew I needed to go to her. I told her that I'd be right there.

She'd gone to the doctor for a checkup. He told her the baby was gone. Atticus had died in the womb. Just wasn't strong enough. He'd fought this long, a scrapper to the end, but it simply wasn't enough. She cried into my chest until it turned dark.

Exhausted from the tears, I scooped her up, carried her to bed, and tucked her in.

For a minute, I watched her peacefully resting, tears dried in veins down her face.

I leaned over her, craned my neck and kissed her on the lips. They were soft and chapped. I never wanted to pull away, but I did.

I laid the roulette wheel on her side table.

That was the last I saw of her.

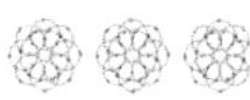

It had been years since that night, but I thought about Robbie virtually every day.

When you truly love someone, they never leave you.

Each time, I picked up a new passenger, I crossed my fingers and prayed to fucking God it was her.

Did I regret it? Of course, I did.

Atticus was going to be ours. A thing we shared. A thing that finally made us whole. And when he died, all of that washed away. Any chance of us being *us* had vanished.

Don't get me wrong. Robbie is, *and was*, the love of my pathetic cab-driving life. But sometimes, you just need to know when it's time to cash out.

For the longest time, I drove around, wondering how she was doing. If she ever settled down. If she found someone who cared for her as much as I did. I'd hope she finally had kids the way she'd wanted. I prayed she was happy.

Last week, a passenger hailed me from the county lock-up. It happened from time to time. Criminals need a ride, too, after all. So, I sat in my shit-heap, waiting in the rain. The name on the Ryde app said Lynn, so when she clamored into the backseat, nobody was more surprised than me.

I hardly recognized her. She'd dyed her hair again. This time jet black, matching her makeup, nails and dress. Her clothes hung on her like she was simply there to keep them upright. She was thin—no fuck that—she was a damn skeleton. Her eyes fell away, sunken; cheeks poking out sharp and gaunt. I didn't know it was her until she spoke, and I heard that old sandpaper song moving past her lips.

"Fucker's stole my rings."

"Sorry?"

"I said, the pigs, they stole my fucking rings." She didn't recognize me and was in too pissy a mood to look me in the eye. I wasn't going to push it.

A reunion seemed out of place. She was still stoned on whatever she was on when they took her in. Her skin pale and clammy. Something about the whole situation scared me.

We drove mostly in silence, but I did happen to get a few words out of her.

"What'd they book you for, if you don't mind me asking?"

"Soliciting and possession. Caught me mid-screw with this fat fucker. Drugs weren't even mine. Like someone in my line of work can afford that much Sniff." She made no qualms about who she was or what she'd done. She was the same old Robbie in that aspect at least.

I dropped her off on Miracle Mile, where the street whores gather because it's well-lit at night. As she stepped out, her eyes narrowed, and she gave me a knowing look. She knew who I was the whole time. She knew who I was and could have cared less.

Robbie took her place with the rest of the gutter trash.

I put my car in gear and drove on.

I guess if you stay in the game long enough, the house always ends up taking their cut.

OFFENDING SHADOWS

If these stories have turned you off,
Listen to my words and philosophe,
Green Valley exists in your mind.
What the hell did you expect to find?
And with so many impossible people living there,
It is now your responsibility to breathe us air.
Without you, our mortal coil is nothing but a wire,
Breathe us the life to which we aspire.
And, while I admit I'm a bit of a schmuck,
I pray you know you can trust in Puck.
You may not have enjoyed every story,
But take a moment for an inventory,
Did we not entertain?
With lessons and humor and sweet love's refrain?
And as you follow the road out of town,
Let it be without a frown.
So as you go and we adjourn,
Please know, we'll be awaiting your return.

ABOUT THE AUTHOR

J. Ryan Sommers has an MFA in creative writing from Columbia College Chicago. He and his wife recently left the windy city and relocated in Houston where Sommers teaches and continues to write.

Sommers has been writing stories since he was a boy. He found it to be an escape at one of the most difficult times of his life, his childhood.

For his efforts he received a Graduate Merit Award from Columbia College Chicago, where he went on to shape the world of *Conduits* and Green Valley.

He has published stories in Zoetic Press, So to Speak, Helen Literary Magazine, Storyfile Magazine, Menda City Press, and The Paragon Review, Here Comes Everyone, and Rotten Tomatoes.

Visit Sommers at his website:
www.jryansommers.weebly.com

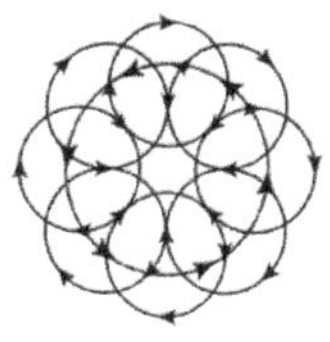

JOIN THE TRANSMUNDANE COMMUNITY

- Find your next favorite read.
- Meet new authors to love.
- Win free books and prizes.
- Play games and join the community contests.
- Watch the latest videos.
- Share the infographics, memes, quizzes, and more!

www.transmundanepress.com
transmundanepress@gmail.com

Made in the USA
Monee, IL
06 February 2020

21390400R00115